Noah pulled his weapon out and crept forward.

Amy had stowed hers in her go bag just in case she was caught alone. US marshals tended to get mad when a protectee tried to help them do their job.

He toed open the door and scanned the woods around the cabin. "It's clear."

Amy felt the hairs on her neck flutter. She stepped outside, then glanced back, wondering if she would ever get the chance to come back here. There were things she wanted. Stuff not required in her bag. She didn't want to lose those things.

A vehicle approached. She heard the crunch of gravel under tires. Then the squeal of brakes.

Noah shoved her back. She fell. Coffee spilled on the entryway rug and his solid body landed on hers.

The rat-a-tat of gunfire cut through the thumping of her heart in her chest.

Noah rolled, taking her past the line of sight in the open doorway while the gunfire continued. He covered her body, arms over her head, so her face was nestled against his shoulder.

Wood splintered around them as the cabin was torn to pieces.

They were going to die.

Lisa Phillips is a British-born, tea-drinking, guitar-playing wife and mom of two. She and her husband lead worship together at their local church. Lisa pens high-stakes stories of mayhem and disaster where you can find made-for-each-other love that always ends in a happily-ever-after. She understands that faith is a work in progress more exciting than any story she can dream up. You can find out more about her books at authorlisaphillips.com.

Jenna Night comes from a family of Southern-born natural storytellers. Her parents were avid readers and the house was always filled with books. No wonder she grew up wanting to tell her own stories. She's lived on both coasts, but currently resides in the inland northwest, where she's astonished by the occasional glimpse of a moose, a herd of elk or a soaring eagle.

COLORADO MANHUNT

LISA PHILLIPS
AND
JENNA NIGHT

⟨H⟩HARLEQUIN®LOVE INSPIRED® SUSPENSE

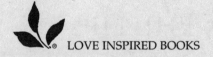

LOVE INSPIRED BOOKS

ISBN-13: 978-1-335-40259-2

Colorado Manhunt

Copyright © 2020 by Harlequin Books S.A.

Wilderness Chase
Copyright © 2020 by Lisa Phillips

Twin Pursuit
Copyright © 2020 by Virginia Niten

www.Harlequin.com

Printed in U.S.A.

CONTENTS

WILDERNESS CHASE

Lisa Phillips

Mega thanks *always* to my writer friends, who drive me to be the best I can be. Couldn't do it without you.

Evil pursueth sinners:
but to the righteous good shall be repayed.
—*Proverbs* 13:21

ONE

Deputy US Marshal Noah Trent glanced in the rearview. Had he lost them? The older SUV had stuck behind him for the past fifty miles of Colorado highway.

Today had been a nightmare from start to finish. First, a prisoner transfer had gone horribly wrong. Now two marshals were dead and three inmates had escaped. He'd hit the road almost as fast as the news had come.

One inmate had been caught, but the other two men were still in the wind. It was assumed they weren't together. Too bad that was about *all* the marshals knew.

If Jeremiah Sanders was loose, it meant one thing. He'd dig up his sister's whereabouts and be at her doorstep faster than you could say, "Incoming."

The man wanted to put his sister, Amy, in the ground as revenge for testifying against him. Then there was the death of Jeremiah's son. Despite what happened to the teen, Jeremiah held her responsible for that, as well. As though she'd been the one to cause the car accident.

Hopefully Jeremiah was still in Washington state, and nowhere near his sister.

Noah looked back for the blue SUV again. He gripped the wheel the same way he'd done all afternoon. Then he tapped the screen of the rental car and listened to the phone ring through the speakers.

"Withers."

Noah said, "It's Deputy Marshal Trent."

"Any problems?"

"An SUV behind me, but I lost them," he told his boss.

"Good," Withers said. "We don't need this turning into more of a circus than it already is."

"Yes, sir."

Withers was all about damage control. Noah didn't fault him, but playing all the angles had to be exhausting. Now that he was within twenty miles of Amy's home, Noah didn't want that SUV to show up again. It would mean leading them right to her.

"Everyone in the Northwest is out looking for those missing inmates." Withers sighed. "I could call the local police to meet you."

"I'm not sure what we could tell them, sir." Noah wasn't about to call in a suspicious SUV without having to explain who she was and why he was here.

Withers said, "They're probably watching for Sanders and Pepperton, anyway, considering the BOLO just went nationwide."

"Good." Noah was glad law enforcement across the country would "be on the lookout" for Jeremiah Sanders and the other escaped prisoner—Richard Pepperton.

"Gotta go," Withers said. "Another case update just came in." He hung up.

Had Jeremiah made his way to Colorado? And how would he even know where to find his sister, considering she was a protected witness? Everyone knew he hated her. Those who hadn't heard him screaming in that courtroom had learned about it from the media coverage.

How much time did Noah have before Jeremiah somehow discovered his sister's whereabouts?

Noah glanced back again to check for the blue SUV. Nothing. Could be cartel foot soldiers following him. Jeremiah had worked with them and was reportedly still doing so in prison. Maybe they'd deployed people all over, looking for Jeremiah or his sister.

Noah would almost rather see the SUV again. Then he could lead it somewhere that was nowhere near Amy's cabin. He wasn't about to put the woman in danger. Noah was going to ignore the fact she fired all his instincts to keep someone safe. Well, obviously that was true since he was a marshal. Keeping people safe was what he did.

But Amy and her huge green eyes, full of fear, just hadn't let go of him. It had been a year since they'd had that…moment. Since they'd almost kissed, and then one of his coworkers had walked in. He should've forgotten about her by now.

Noah sighed, a reply to the hum of the tires on the road. He'd vowed a long time ago that relationships weren't for him if he wanted to make director before he was fifty. There were too many people who needed protecting, and he couldn't be distracted by a woman he wouldn't know for long before she faded out of his life.

Again.

Noah checked his rearview once more before the turn-off to her cabin. He drove down the gravel road, past the vacation cabins. A couple of cars were parked outside.

It was another six miles to Amy's place. When the marshal in charge of her case had securely sent him the location, simply because he was closer, Noah hadn't been able to believe the city girl would be so far from anywhere.

Then he saw it. Her cabin, nestled in a clearing. Single story. Probably one bedroom. Boards on the outside had been replaced, the varnish on those planks a slightly different shade than the rest. Floral drapes. Empty flowerpots on the porch.

She needed a rocker.

The idea of getting one for her made his lips curl into a smile. He parked and trotted to her front door, energized by the idea of seeing her. Seemed a shame to make her leave, but he could get her back here to her nice cabin soon enough. It was the exact kind of place he'd love to go on vacation. If he ever took one.

Noah knocked on the front door, and it creaked open. His other hand readied to pull his gun. He had to be prepared for anything.

"Amy? It's the US Marshals." He could get to who he was soon enough, when she knew she was safe.

He stepped inside and looked around. Tiny kitchen, rustic furniture that looked more comfortable than his. The TV had been left on.

Paused.

The screen showed a prison picture of Jeremiah and the other man, both still at large. Presumed extremely dangerous. Across the bottom of the screen it read Call Police Immediately.

Noah called out, "Amy!" again.

No answer.

He walked through the cabin, checking for her in the bathroom and bedroom. His pace quickened as he went, as each second ticked by and he didn't find her. The mudroom at the back was piled up with boots, shoes and tennis shoes. Jackets and sweaters hung, and the back door was wide open.

She wasn't here.

Noah stood on the step at the back door and yelled, "Amy!"

* * *

Amy gripped the gun in trembling fingers, crouched behind a downed tree. She knew that voice.

It was Noah.

Relief rushed through her, but hot on its heels was the realization that she couldn't be certain she could trust him. Right now she wasn't certain she could trust *anyone*.

She bit her lip. Seeing her brother's face on the TV, and then hearing the car out front, she'd fumbled with the remote before dropping it. There had only been time to grab the gun and run out the back door. No panic to cloud her thinking, which meant she was already outside running across the frozen grass of the lawn before she even thought to get shoes. Now that the adrenaline had dissipated she could think straight.

Amy stood. She held the gun in front of her and gingerly wandered in his direction. "Noah?"

Even if he meant to hurt her, she could shoot him. Right? Okay, probably not, given their history. She tried to act strong, but it wasn't like she could actually get over the fear that liked to paralyze her. She'd thought her days of facing down her brother were over.

Now all that had come rushing back with one word. *Escaped.*

"Amy!" He trotted over as she made her way to him. The look of worry on his face helped. He scanned her, head to toe. "You ran outside with no coat, and no shoes?"

Only then did she realize that under the sleeves of her shirt gooseflesh prickled her skin. She had a short-sleeved T-shirt on over a long-sleeved undershirt. That was something, at least. But with skinny jeans and wool socks, it wasn't much protection against the frigid temperatures.

"There was no time," she argued. "I thought you were

Jeremiah." She would have left that spot where she'd been hiding and run deeper into the brush if it had been anyone but Noah. She didn't even trust the marshal assigned to her case.

His gaze softened further. "Let's get you inside."

She nodded. Her socks were wet, making her toes numb. "I just put a pot of coffee on."

"We can turn it off before we leave."

She glanced over at him, slowing her pace. "I'm not leaving." He wasn't just here to brief her? She'd assumed he would hang out here until her brother was caught. Make sure nothing happened to her.

Amy shivered at the idea that her brother might actually find her. Didn't Witness Security—which most people knew as the witness protection program—have measures in place to keep that from happening? It was hard to believe that in a matter of hours after escaping from federal custody, her brother would be able to locate her *and* reach her doorstep.

She didn't want to ask, but had to. "Is there something I don't know?"

Noah said, "Let's get inside. You're shivering."

"I'm not all that worried about being cold, considering there's a murderous maniac on the loose." Even after all this time she didn't like referring to her brother that way. But there was little point in refusing to accept reality.

She stepped inside, and he shut the door behind them. "You have a bag ready?"

"My 'go' bag?" That was for emergencies. "Is Jeremiah on his way here?"

Noah lifted one shoulder. "The truth is we have no idea where he is. So the quicker you can get a coat, shoes and your bag, the faster we can get out of here. There's a safe house set up."

"This was supposed to be my safe house." She had to say it. Even though arguing was futile, she had to voice those things. Tiny flashes of defiance against everything Jeremiah had put her through.

Yes, it had been her choice to testify against him. But it had been the right thing. Otherwise who knew what destruction he would've caused in the end? Or how many lives might have been lost.

He'd told her he was trying to find a job so he could get on his feet, and properly support his son. She'd gotten him a cell phone on her plan so prospective employers could contact him. A few weeks later, when he hadn't said anything to her about any interviews, she'd looked at his texts on her online account.

That was when she'd discovered the truth. Jeremiah had been transporting drugs and guns for a cartel.

It had broken her heart. What else could she have done when feds showed up at her doorstep except turn everything over to the FBI?

Amy got clean socks and put a pair of boots on. She added a sweater, even though she was going to put her thick coat on. Gloves and a scarf. A hat. She'd gotten used to Colorado winters, and loved the chill in the air, but the cold set in fast no matter how "used to it" she was. Her "go" bag had a packet of those hand warmers in it, the ones she liked to slip inside her gloves when she went snowshoeing.

"Ready?" Noah had two insulated tumblers out. He replaced the carafe and topped one tumbler up with cold water—he took his coffee black. Amy got her bag while he put milk in hers and screwed the lid on. He walked out of the kitchen. "No sense wasting good coffee."

He handed one tumbler to her, leaving one of his hands

free. She shot him a look. "How do you know I don't buy the cheap stuff?"

They headed for the door, and she saw his shiver. "Don't even joke about that." Car keys jingled against the tumbler as he walked. At the front door, he waved her to the side. No smiles.

She knew the drill.

Noah pulled his weapon out. She'd stowed hers in her "go" bag just in case she was caught alone. In her experience, US Marshals tended to get mad when a protectee tried to help them do their job.

He toed open the door and scanned. "It's clear."

Amy felt the hairs on her neck flutter. She stepped outside, then glanced back. Would she ever get the chance to return here? There were things she wanted. Stuff not required in her bag, but which still meant something to her. She didn't want to lose the things she'd chosen. Just as she didn't want to lose the life she'd started to build for herself here over the past year.

Jeremiah was ruining everything. Again.

A vehicle approached. She heard the crunch of gravel under tires, followed by the squeal of brakes.

Noah shoved her back. Coffee spilled on the entryway rug and his solid body landed on hers. Tackled to the floor. Because her brother was *trying to kill her.*

The rat-a-tat of automatic gunfire cut through the thump of her heart in her chest.

Noah rolled her past the line of sight in the open doorway while the gunfire continued. He covered her body. Arms over her head, so her face was nestled against his shoulder.

Wood splintered around them as the cabin was torn to pieces.

They were going to die.

TWO

He heard her whimper, but there was no time for comfort. Air rushed in his ears and he could feel wet under one knee. Spilled coffee.

"Come on." He hauled her up and they moved.

Through the house, toward the back door. The hallway would put them in the line of fire. Noah stopped at the doorway from the kitchen to the hall and peered around the frame. The gunshots had stopped. Would one of the men come around to the back door, to try and cut off their escape?

His brain wanted to run through all those lingering questions... Who were these guys? How had they found the cabin? But dwelling on all that would only get them killed. Right now they needed to move.

Beyond the open front door—and Amy's "go" bag that she'd dropped—was a blue SUV. The same one that had been behind him on the highway a while ago. It had to be, because in his experience there was no such thing as a coincidence. Not when it came down to protecting witnesses. But he'd lost that vehicle. They hadn't followed him here.

Amy clutched his arm. He could hear her breath coming fast. She was scared, relying on him to keep her safe

and get them both out of there. The weight of that responsibility was heavy, but not unwelcome. It was the
career he'd chosen, the path on which he felt the most
like himself.

"Stay here." He tugged her to stand right up against
the wall, where he'd been. "When I say, you run out the
back door. Okay?"

She nodded, wide eyes full of fear.

Noah moved back the way they'd come. Both men
were still outside. One watching the cabin, the other on
a phone. Calling in the fact that they had found Amy? He
didn't like the idea of more men showing up.

Noah reached out with his foot and kicked the front
door shut, then ducked to the side. Gunshots peppered
the wood as he fired two shots through the window, oblit-
erating the glass and screen.

He ran for the back door. They could get out, it was
clear. Both men were out front and waiting...for whatever it
was they were waiting for. Noah wasn't going to do that.

He and Amy were getting out of there.

"Go, Amy! Now!" he called out loud enough she could
hear, but not so loud it would be audible from out front.

In a flash of the dark material of her jacket, he saw
her run.

Noah caught up at the back door just as she pulled it
open. Amy stepped back and to the side, and he moved
around her. If he'd explained what he wanted her to do,
there was no way it would have come out that smoothly.
Thank You, God. They moved as though he'd protected
her for years. And in a way, he had. He'd just been doing
it from afar since the trial.

A whole year.

Now they met like this?

Noah exited first, gun up. Amy tapped his shoulder.

"Come on." He grabbed her hand and they ran for the trees.

Snow lay a couple of feet deep around the cabin. Amy steered them to a trodden-down path, crunchy rutted snow she'd apparently walked frequently.

The cold air chilled his hands, and the material of her glove over the hand he held. He picked up their pace as they headed along the path. They would be out in the open until they got to the tree line. How far did her path go? And where did it lead?

He was about to ask her when she said, "Careful of—"

Noah's foot hit a patch of slick snow and he stumbled. His leg gave out, and his knee hit hard-packed snow. He grunted, but held the reaction back.

"You okay?"

He nodded and got his feet under him. He kept running, still holding her hand. He'd probably squeezed it to death for a second there, when his brain had realized his body was falling. Noah kept scanning the area as they ran. Waiting for the second when those gunmen figured out they'd escaped out the back and set off in pursuit.

Thankfully, the ground was so frozen they weren't making any tracks on the rutted path. Unfortunately, however, that meant his knee throbbed with every step.

He gritted his teeth and pushed on.

"You're not okay." Her voice came out breathy.

"Doesn't matter." Maybe she was scared, and sympathy gave her something to think about beyond the fear. Whatever the reason, he liked that she cared. What he didn't like was that they weren't at the tree line yet.

A shot rang out.

Amy squealed. They both ducked and pressed on, running hunched over. They couldn't veer from the path or they'd be wading in snow. Noah ran as hard and fast as he could, praying with every step that neither of them slipped.

The second he passed the first tree, he entertained the idea they might make it. Noah sucked in a breath. Tried to calm his exhale. Otherwise he was going to end up passing out.

The pathway angled to the east, and they ran along it.

He slowed, turned as he ran. Checked behind them. Those men were coming. "Where does this go?"

"Into town."

Would they make it that far?

Amy wanted to whimper. What would giving in to the fear accomplish? That hadn't helped during the trial. It wouldn't help now, when her brother was coming after her. Whether that meant he would show up here in person, or send men to abduct her, she didn't know. Could be he'd only escaped in order to force the marshals to show up at her house. All part of his plan to get revenge on her.

Use the marshals to flush her out, and then kill her.

Without her bag, which she'd dropped before they ran out, Amy had exactly one thing that might keep her alive. But revealing her secret to her brother meant putting an innocent person in danger. It was the last thing she wanted to do, despite the fact it could save her life.

Could she die to protect her nephew's life?

Absolutely.

In a way, she already had. The person she used to be had perished. Now she was…someone entirely different, living an entirely different life hundreds of miles from who she was. Hundreds of miles from wherever Anthony was.

They ran at least another two miles until she saw the tree. Gnarled and crusty, it had been hit by lightning.

Split in two. She liked to sit on it and rest, on her way into or coming home from town.

A couple of times a month, Amy walked to church. Or for a slice of pie from the diner. In summer she did it a lot more. This time of year it was harder to get around. She'd been thinking about an ATV. Too late now. Would have come in handy today, though.

"You okay?"

She glanced over. "You're the one limping."

"Don't worry about me."

"Going to play the stoic hero, protecting the damsel in distress?"

He shot her a look. "Not a cliché if it's actually what's happening." He shrugged. "This is where we are. We can either complain, or we can figure out how to get to a vehicle."

"I was thinking more like go to the sheriff's office."

"Does he know who you really are?"

She rolled her eyes. "Of course not. That's why you're here, right?" He didn't say anything then, just scanned the area around them. She didn't believe they'd lost those guys. Only that they'd gotten far enough ahead running flat out that they had a second to catch their breath.

Then she saw them out the corner of her eye.

"We should—"

He didn't need to finish. Amy said, "Hide."

"I was going to say 'go.' But 'hide' works." He followed her around to the back of the tree. It was big enough that it should conceal them until these guys moved on. Then maybe they could go back to the cabin, and Noah's car.

Amy watched as the two gunmen came into view. They both looked around, and then the other gunman pulled out a phone. No, not a phone. That one had a radio.

"Probably checking in," Noah whispered, crouched beside her. He tugged his cell from his pocket, and she saw him send a text message. Or try to. "I have no signal."

The gunman on the phone looked to be having problems, too. He looked at the screen of his phone, clearly frustrated.

Amy leaned closer to him. "Should we make a run for it?"

Noah shook his head. "We're safer out of sight. For now. Hiding was a good idea." He turned to watch the two men, and she got the chance to look at his face in profile.

Strong features. He probably thought his ears were too big, but she'd always thought they fit his face. She wondered what he'd looked like as a kid. If he'd gone through that awkward phase everyone seemed to have around middle school, and into high school. Then again, maybe he'd always been like this.

Steady. Protective. He'd probably had a best friend he'd helped keep safe from bullies. Or a neighborhood kid. Like that boy with Down syndrome on her street when she'd been growing up. She'd loved handing out candy on Halloween, just because he would come and she'd get to see him smile like it was Christmas.

"Amy."

She blinked away the memories. "What?"

He pointed over her shoulder. She turned, facing the fact she couldn't live in her memories. The good times were long gone. Nothing in her life right now was even close to that, even though she'd been working hard to be happy. Or at least trying to find some piece of "happy."

On the opposite side of where they crouched, huddled behind the tree, two more men approached. Gunmen, or hunters? It could hardly be a coincidence that more gunmen happened to find them here.

Had her brother sent a whole army to find her? And how was it that they seemed to be closing in on their hiding spot? These gunmen had to know where she and Noah were somehow, which meant they couldn't stay here.

She turned back to him, ready to tell him that.

"Time to run." He didn't look happy about it, but if he thought they should do it, then she was going to. Noah would go with what he thought would keep her alive. She was trusting him to keep them both alive.

Amy shifted around, ready to sprint, and saw that look in his eyes. One she'd seen a few times, all of them a year ago during the trial. A look that said he cared more than he was going to say about her.

She looked away from it now, because it wasn't going to help. During the trial she'd let those thoughts distract her. They'd been a nice distraction, taking a few seconds in the middle of the insanity to think about what might have been. Right now it wasn't going to help. Not when the reality was that their lives were incompatible. He was a marshal. She was a witness living in seclusion.

Who knew if they would even survive today?

THREE

With every step into the snow, Noah wondered if it would be their last. Would their bodies be found in spring, when the snow melted? He couldn't help the shudder as they trudged. Quietly. As quick as they could. Crouched down, wading through the snow.

Trying not to get shot.

"Which way is town?" His phone wasn't loading the Maps app, so he had no idea where they were. Let alone where they were going.

"That way." She pointed left, her arm angled behind her at the seven o'clock position.

"But…"

"Come on. I know where we can go."

Noah frowned, but continued to follow. If he argued with her it could draw attention to them. They were far too exposed as it was. Essentially crawling through the brush and snow trying to get away from gunmen in the woods searching for them.

"Hey!"

The cry rang out. Snow drifted from the branches of a tree. It was beautiful, if it wasn't going to be the last thing he saw before he was killed, before Amy was taken by hired guns and delivered to her brother to be executed.

"Go!" He hauled her to her feet and they ran.

Shots resounded through the forest, the sound harsh and far too loud out here in the still winter of the Colorado wilderness.

Noah spun around and fired back. A gunman fell.

He caught up to Amy and they kept going, tearing through the trees. He had no idea where they were headed but had to rely on her knowledge of this area. Presumably she'd hiked it. Maybe she'd even prepared for an eventuality such as this. Witnesses were counseled about the possible need for escape plans. Hopefully she'd taken the marshals service's advice and done it well. He wanted to believe that. To trust her. But only time would tell. Noah had to do what was best for her.

Whether or not she liked it, or agreed with him, there may come a point when he had to make a choice.

If he was going to die for anyone—as much as he didn't want to think about that—then he would rather it was her than someone else.

Just Amy.

A couple more shots rang out. Farther away this time.

He looked back and saw two guys in an argument. Whatever that was about, he didn't know. But he thanked God for it and kept running.

Maybe they'd been ordered not to kill Amy, but to abduct her instead? Or none of them liked the idea of killing a US Marshal. Whatever the reason they were arguing and not racing after the two people fleeing, he wasn't going to object.

"This way." Amy changed directions.

Hopefully they could get far enough, fast enough, those guys would lose them. But he'd thought that with the SUV on the highway and the vehicle had pulled up at Amy's cabin.

As though they knew exactly where she was.

Like maybe he had led them there.

Noah pulled out his phone. No signal, which meant he wasn't being tracked. Possibly they could've tracked his phone to the cabin. Someone at the marshals service would've had to have leaked the information that it was him headed to her. Or they'd been hacked.

Seemed like they were doing a coordinated search now. Pinning them down out here. They would probably leave Noah bleeding in the snow and take Amy.

"You okay?"

"Yeah." Why wouldn't he be? His knee hurt, but that wasn't the point. "Why?"

"You made a funny noise."

Was he supposed to tell her that the thought of being left for dead while she was taken was like how he imagined the sudden realization that he'd been shoved off a cliff would feel? He didn't even know if he could put it into words. Let alone do that while they were on the run.

He'd try and explain later, if they got the chance. Until then, he'd have to make sure that didn't happen.

Noah glanced back but couldn't see anyone in pursuit. "I'm fine. Just go…wherever we're going." Up ahead a cabin came into view. "That?"

"It's a hunting cabin." They jogged over to it.

"They'll know we're in here as soon as they see it."

"I know." She didn't stop. "But there's a radio in there. And supplies."

A couple minutes to stop, and then they moved on? "Let's be quick."

He halted her at the front door. Noah scanned outside, then went in first. He kept her in sight at all times. When he'd looked in, sure there was no one waiting, he waved her to enter. Then shut the door.

"Don't turn on any of the lights—"

She finished for him. "And stay away from the windows."

Amy knew the drill. A fact he appreciated, about as much as he didn't like that it was necessary. She had the tools. She'd been through this before, and during the trial. That would help keep both of them safe now.

She was the kind of person who deserved to have a peaceful, safe life. Not one where she was constantly on the run, scared because her brother wanted to kill her.

If he hadn't escaped…

Dreaming that it hadn't happened wasn't going to help. Wishful thinking, or denial, wouldn't keep the bullets from flying at them. It didn't matter what he thought her life should have been, or the good a person like Amy deserved. After all, she'd done the right thing. The place they were right now, and the situation they were in, took precedence.

She held the receiver of a radio in her hand.

"What is it?" Noah walked over. "Is it not working?"

Maybe they'd killed the radio signal somehow. His cell didn't have any bars. He'd figured this middle of nowhere wilderness was just one of those dead spots. A broken radio on top of that?

"It's just…" The fear hadn't left those bright green eyes of hers. "What if they're listening? They'll know where we are when I tell the sheriff."

"Tell the sheriff." He jerked his thumb in the direction of the door. "Then we're out of here before they can show up."

He turned and looked around while she got on the radio and spoke with the dispatcher. He searched for anything useful they could take with them. This was like some kind of communal cabin. A place to crash after a long day of hunting, all the things here common use. Take one, leave one of something else. A cooperative effort to stay out of the weather without hauling in a tent or it costing money.

If they had to stay here, they could. But it wasn't safe—not when there were gunmen in the area.

They had to keep moving.

"Thank you." She replaced the handset on the table-top and turned, her stomach a ball of knots. She wanted the distraction of gathering up her bag but didn't even have that.

"Ready?"

She nodded. "They're going to have someone meet us on the highway. If those men are listening in somehow, then we'll have to find a place to hide."

Behind a tree again? That had worked before, but she didn't like the idea of being pinned down waiting for death. It seemed like that had happened several times since Noah had shown up.

She wanted to run again, holding his hand. Amy wasn't a coward. She couldn't have done what she'd done and testified against a whole cartel if she had been. She'd have caved when the first death threats came in.

She'd been alone for a year now, trying to figure out how to trust people. How to not give in to the fear and let it swallow her whole. Sure, she'd basically retreated. She rode her bicycle or walked to work, interacting with her boss and their customers at the bookstore. She knew how to make a fabulous caramel macchiato that Noah would probably think was way too sweet. But she never connected with people.

She wasn't ready yet.

Or she hadn't been, until Noah showed up in the snow.

Someone moved past the window.

Amy swallowed back a scream. Choked on it. Noah spun from her to the window, putting her behind him. Whoever walked through the door would meet him first. Their bullets would *hit* him first.

It was enough to make her drown in the fear. That mental image of him falling. The blood.

A whimper worked its way up her throat. She shoved it back down. Why did she have to react like that every time? If she wasn't about to be killed she might try to work on being braver, but there wasn't time.

She looked around for a weapon. Her gaze snagged on a latch…on the floor.

Noah had his weapon out. She crouched and grasped at the latch. Pulled it up and open. A trapdoor. Inside were wooden stairs leading down. "I think this is an old root cellar, or something." They could hide inside.

Behind him, boots pounded on the front steps.

"Come on," she whispered.

He had to hurry, or they would be found. Not waiting for him, Amy stumbled down the steps. One hand out straight, she slammed it into a wall. Dirt. This was an old root cellar, like an Old West refrigerator. And it was freezing down here.

A second later Noah followed. He pulled the trapdoor shut over their heads.

Shut in.

Totally dark. *Oh, no.*

She'd tried so hard to work past it, but she could feel it coming now. Breath hitched in her throat. Each inhale faster than the previous one. Hands reached for her. Grasped her sleeve. Then she felt a hand run from her elbow down to her wrist. He tugged her to him, gently.

"Amy." He whispered her name.

Each breath wasn't enough. Amy tried to suck in a lungful of air, but it hitched halfway. She was making too much noise.

Why did this have to happen now? There was no way it should come on this fast. She'd been working on it. Trying to get past it.

Noah's shirt was warm. His strong hand rubbed up and down her back. "Shhh."

He knew. He'd been one of the marshals that had raided the house along with FBI agents in full tactical gear. Law enforcement personnel who had rescued her before her brother's friends could hand her over to be killed.

Where is our money?

She squeezed her eyes shut and wound her arms around Noah now. This was what was happening right here, in the present.

She wasn't in that house. There were no gunmen down here in this cellar. Just her and Noah. The marshal who had come to keep her safe, so that the terror she'd gone through before didn't happen again.

Amy worked to push down the panic. Nothing but a memory. A reaction, a symptom in her recovery. Not even a setback. She wasn't going to let it have that much power over her.

He held her tight. A hug that was every bit as strong and reassuring as it was when he'd held her hand. When he stood in front of her to meet the danger first.

Above their heads boards creaked. Those booted feet, walking around inside the cabin.

Amy held herself still. They were right above them.

One sound, and she and Noah would be killed.

FOUR

Noah tried to reassure her, but couldn't use words. The man above them would surely hear if he even made the tiniest sound. Amy had been having a panic attack. Because of the dark enclosed space?

The footsteps above moved through the cabin as the person looked around. Noah prayed they wouldn't find the trapdoor, despite it being in the middle of the floor. If they weren't discovered, it would be for sure a God-thing.

Noah trusted in Him to keep them safe. He also prayed for Amy. She needed to hold it together and not let the fear overtake her. Right before the trial she'd been under marshal guard at a hotel. During transport to where she'd been supposed to record a video of her testimony for the US Attorney, they'd been ambushed.

Amy had been taken.

Three hours later, he'd been part of the team that stormed the house and got her back. The cartel foot soldiers who'd been holding her were either killed in the operation, or sent to jail and killed there. Far too convenient. None of them had ever given anything away.

As for Noah, he would never forget the look on her face when he'd kicked the basement door in and found her tied to that chair. They'd saved her that day, but clearly there were lasting repercussions. The fact she was able to keep a lid on her reaction, enough to not give away their hiding spot, was a good sign. She'd retained that strength he'd seen in her during the trial. That resolve to do the right thing.

A door slammed above.

Amy flinched in his arms. He squeezed her hands and let her go so she could take a half step back.

He whispered, "Keep quiet for a little longer, okay?"

"Okay." Her voice was small. Forlorn.

He'd liked to have hugged her again, but that would be more about reassuring himself that she was all right. Amy was his protectee. He shouldn't move things beyond what was professional. A year ago, during the trial, he'd still been a newer agent. He was more seasoned now, but he could still remember every word of his boss's caution against allowing his personal feelings for Amy to interfere with his career.

Getting tangled with a witness will mark you until you retire. You'll be that *deputy and you'll never shake it.*

He could care about her. He could protect her.

What he couldn't do was fall for her.

Noah shifted to face the stairs and felt his way up a couple of steps until he could touch the trapdoor above his head. "I need to go and see if the coast is clear. Stay here."

She said nothing.

"Amy?"

He heard her sniff. Then she said, "Okay."

Noah needed to do this safely, but also quickly. She needed to get out of this dark, enclosed space and out where she could see daylight.

He prayed again, and held his breath as he listened for noise on the other side of the trapdoor. When he heard nothing for another minute except the distant sound of a small engine, he eased it up. No time to lose. They could have been forced to stay in that cellar for hours, but the sheriff's department wasn't coming here. He didn't know if Amy could handle being down there that long. The situation could get worse in that time, not better.

An inch of sunlight spilled in. He listened again and thought he might have heard Amy whisper, "Please be careful."

She was scared, but knowing she cared about him helped. It made him a little bit more confident that she wouldn't put them both at risk. Some witnesses didn't listen. But the fact was, Witness Security hadn't lost a protectee who followed their rules. That was why they had them in place.

Noah eased the trapdoor all the way open and laid it down as carefully as he could. If the wood banged the floor someone might come running.

He climbed out and moved to the window, staying out of sight as he looked around. A man climbed behind another onto the back of a snowmobile. They roared off and he realized the one on the back had been the man he'd shot at Amy's cabin.

Taken away because he needed medical attention, maybe.

So where were the other two?

He moved through the cabin and looked out the other windows. Tried to see where the gunmen had gone. Finally, he spotted them. "There you are."

Before either could turn and see him through the window, he ducked out of sight again. If he was going to take them out, he needed to do it without using his gun. The noise of a gunshot would carry through the snowy wilderness. Every gunman in the area—and he didn't figure these four were out here alone—would be drawn to them.

Noah walked to the front door, determined to get this done. He kicked the side table as he went. Two empty drink cans clattered to the floor. A second later, someone yelled outside.

Noah swiped up one of the metal folding chairs that sat around the card table and adjusted his grip. *Here goes nothin'.* He'd need to swing it hard and fast to take the men down without getting shot.

Footsteps pounded around to the front door. Noah watched the door handle rotate, counting every breath as he braced for what was about to happen.

The first man stepped in. Noah waited a heartbeat and then swung with the chair. It slammed into the man's face and shoulders. He dropped to the floor.

The momentum took the chair into the door. Noah tried to pull the swing, but it slammed the wood. The impact rushed up his arm.

It wouldn't be long before the other man stepped in.

Out the corner of his eye, he saw movement. But it wasn't the other man. It was Amy, coming out of the cellar.

The expression on Noah's face didn't mean anything good.

She looked at the man on the floor. "Wow, he—"

Noah's gun came up. *Pointed right at her.* "No!"

Arms banded around her and lifted her feet off the ground. Amy tried to scream but the air caught in her throat as this man's arm pressed against her diaphragm.

"Let her go!" Noah's voice rang through the cabin.

Her head swam. She kicked with her legs. Tried to hit back at the man holding her. Fresh from a panic attack, she had little in the way of reserves. But the last thing she wanted was to be taken from here.

"Gun down!" The man's voice was heavily accented. She'd heard that lilt before, but couldn't be sure if it had been this man specifically.

Where is our money?

Her gaze connected with Noah's. She could see the intent there in his eyes, plain as if he'd spoken the words out loud. He would die to save her.

Noah's lips pressed together for a second, and she saw a slight shake of his head. "No way. I'm not lowering my gun."

Nothing about what he'd said surprised her. He was a federal agent, and he wasn't about to disarm himself. Especially not with a witness in the room in danger.

The gunman shifted his aim. He laid his forearm on her shoulder, weapon pointed at Noah.

She could try and shove it away.

Noah gave another tiny shift of his head. Didn't like her idea? Apparently she was broadcasting it on her face and he'd seen it.

Too bad the alternative was that these men shoot each other. And she was between them, just standing here waiting to get hit.

Instead of keeping watch on that take-charge thing he had going, she shut her eyes. Yes, he was the marshal and she was the protected witness. That didn't mean she had to be helpless, did it?

She heard the gunman's ragged breathing. Felt the squeeze of his arm, still holding her waist tight.

The weight of his arm rested on her shoulder and tugged it down. She wanted to shake it off. Not helpful. She needed to get out of his grip instead, move away from being between Noah and the target he wanted to hit. She couldn't turn to the left—he'd just hold on tighter. She needed to spin right. Into the arm holding her.

Amy opened her eyes. She motioned to the right with her gaze, and then she moved. Turned to the inside of his arm. It shifted with his surprise. Amy moved to the side, so the back of her shoulder faced Noah. Body out of the way. She did it fast enough that Noah used those few seconds before the gunman realized what was happening.

A shot cracked through the room. The noise was deafening in the small space.

Amy's entire body flinched. She shoved the gunman's arm away, praying she didn't get shot in the back of the head for her trouble.

He let go. His hand fell away and he hit the floor behind her.

Dead.

Noah grabbed Amy's hand. "Come on." He grabbed the gunman's weapon and tugged her to the door. "We have to get out of here before someone who heard that shot shows up."

She nodded, hardly able to process everything.

Yes, he'd saved her life. He'd also *taken* a life. His job. Was it supposed to hit her like this?

"You okay?"

They were at the door now. She nodded, even though tears rolled down her face. Beside the door were snowshoes, stacked upright. "Let's take these." They could cut across the snow and make it to the road, avoiding anyone else that might be out there looking for them.

She handed him a pair, not acknowledging the look on his face. She had to push aside emotion and face the next step. The next heartbeat, the next breath. That was all. Just stick with the basics. Keep her head together. Don't get caught in that undertow, the residual effects of the panic attack causing everything to be so close to the surface.

Noah led the way outside where they put snowshoes on. "If we need to run, can we do it in these?"

"You have to be careful, but you should be able to run."

"Do you want this gun?"

She looked down at the weapon in his hand, the gunman's weapon. After a second of debate she took it, hit the button to slide the clip out. It was nearly empty. Because the gunman had shot at her when they'd been back at her cabin? She shoved it back in and pulled back the slide.

Noah said, "Okay, let's go."

He set off. She wanted him to take her hand again, but she couldn't rely on him to support her. She had to stand by herself. All those things she'd believed she could do. Now she was actually having to do them. Self-defense. Weapons training.

Running.

No one out for a jog ever believed it was only training for the next time they had to run for their life.

Except her.

Noah scanned the area as he walked. "I saw two of them take off on a snowmobile. One is dead back there, and the other is unconscious."

"He'll probably wake up and come after us, right?" She glanced back at the hunting cabin and shuddered. Not just because of the man lying on the floor by the door. She never wanted to be anywhere near that place after everything that had happened in there.

The marshals wouldn't ever let her come back to this area, anyway. They would relocate her. A new name. A new life.

Noah said, "All the more reason to pick up the pace."

Amy followed him, her mind full of the knowledge that every step she took might be her last.

Her brother was coming for her.

FIVE

The snowshoes were awkward, but Noah couldn't deny they made better progress across the mountainside, through the trees and two-feet-deep snow, a whole lot faster with them than without. Both of them would have had wet pant legs, and they'd be even more cold now.

"Is that a car up ahead?"

He took a few more steps, trying to see what she'd been referring to. Despite the markings denoting it as a county sheriff's vehicle, he said, "Wait here for a second." Then he did a half walk, half run in snowshoes to the side of the highway, where a sheriff's department vehicle waited.

Just the small SUV. No occupant.

"Okay." He waved her over.

Tension sat like a knot in his stomach. Like a bad case of food poisoning.

They had to get help.

Noah's whole body was covered in a sheen of sweat. He felt like he'd run his usual morning routine of six miles, but all of it uphill. He estimated they'd maybe walked three miles, if that. It felt so much farther with the extra exertion of wading through Colorado winter in snowshoes.

He blew out a breath. Amy came over to him. She was maybe a little winded but didn't seem any worse for their…workout. That sounded a whole lot better than running for their lives.

"Where is the sheriff?"

Noah looked around. Then he walked across the hard-packed snow on the road to circle the SUV. The snowshoes didn't help when the snow was matted down like ice, but if he took them off and more gunmen came, how would he get them back on? Mostly he figured he'd regret it if he took them off and he'd probably regret leaving them on.

Useful, but not exactly user-friendly.

Noah tugged on the driver's door handle. "It's unlocked." He saw the state of the interior. "Not good."

"What is it?"

He lifted a hand. "Stay over there." He wanted her to have at least a chance of cover to hide behind, and she was closer to the trees on that side of the vehicle.

"What is it?" Her tone was different this time, heavy with a hint of what he'd seen when she'd opened her eyes. Right before she'd twisted out of the gunman's arms. The determination inside her, not just to do the right thing but also to pull her weight. To treat this like a partnership, and not like he was the marshal and she was the witness.

Noah wouldn't let anyone else make that shift. Amy? He trusted her. She did what he needed her to. She followed orders. She also showed him that vulnerable side he wanted to take care of.

"Noah."

"There's blood on the seat."

"How much?"

She really wanted the answer to that? "Enough he's light-headed, but hopefully still alive."

She twisted around to look at the area. "Do you think he's here somewhere, hurt?"

"Whoever injured him took the time to shut the door after they got him out of the SUV."

"So they dragged him off and left him in the snow to bleed out and die? Or he was already dead?"

Was she angling for a job as a detective? "When we find him, or whoever hurt him, we can ask them." He took a step back. If the sheriff—or whoever had shown up—left the vehicle bleeding, wouldn't there be blood on the snow somewhere? He didn't see any. Not losing blood meant the wound was either not bleeding now or had been staunched somehow. A stray drop would be here, surely.

The alternative was that the person had died before they were moved—no more blood flow to get on the snow.

He shook his head. Now he was doing exactly what he accused her of doing—trying to figure out what happened with no evidence.

Noah wandered to the far side of the empty highway. He looked for footprints. Probably more than one person had been out here. Where were they?

Behind him, he heard the other door to the SUV open. Heard Amy's intake of breath. Exactly what he hadn't wanted her to see, that visible evidence of injury. Something to trigger another panic attack.

She'd done well to keep it together so far. He didn't want to be the cause of something she wouldn't be able to fight off. A rush of emotion that would slow them down.

Then he spotted something.

"Over here!"

He called out before he even realized what he'd done. Noah rushed to the sheriff's deputy's side, landing awkwardly on his knees because of the snowshoes. "Can you hear me?"

He patted the man's cheek, not looking at the blood on his shoulder. The law officer seemed to have passed out, his shoulder bundled up by his jacket. Why leave the vehicle, though? Walking off to pass out in the snow didn't seem like a good idea.

He drew his gun. Then he grabbed the uniformed man's good arm and hauled the man onto his back. Noah stood up from his crouch and faced Amy. "Get back to the SUV. Try to find some keys."

He followed her, carrying the man over his shoulder. Teeth gritted. Each footstep a prayer that he wouldn't trip over the edge of one of these shoe-things and fall.

She got in the front seat. "You think someone is here, like, watching?"

He hauled open the back door. "Maybe." Then laid the uniformed man on the back seat. Noah didn't figure his chances were good if they didn't get him to a hospital, or whatever passed for one in this town, and quick.

The engine cranked. Coughed, then turned over. He ran around to the passenger door and got in.

Amy tossed her snowshoes on the floor in the back and then threw the SUV in Drive.

"Go."

She hit the gas. "Where?"

Noah looked around. He'd expected someone to come out of the woods and murder them. Leaving the officer for them to find like that… It didn't make any sense.

"You think that was a trap?"

He nodded. She saw it out the corner of her eye as she drove toward the medical center, which was thankfully on this end of town.

"You think he'll be okay?"

"I hope so."

She knew he wouldn't like it if a law enforcement person was killed. Not when his job here was protection. She was the one he was supposed to be keeping safe—and alive—but she knew firsthand how they felt about collateral damage. And how deeply they reacted to the loss of what they'd refer to as "one of their own."

"If it was a trap," she said, "wouldn't they have waited for us to show up?"

"I'd have thought so."

"Or hurt him." She jabbed at the back seat with her thumb. "And taken his car?" Except they hadn't, and now she was the one driving it. None of this made sense.

"Maybe that was the plan, and then they got called away. Like to the cabin. Could be we crossed paths—or we would have if we hadn't been cutting across the forest in these snowshoes." He put his with hers, in the footwell of the back seat.

"How are we supposed to figure out what the answer is?"

He shifted and pulled the cell phone from his back pocket. "Still no signal."

"It'll be a minute until we get closer to town. Unless you have the one carrier that literally gets zero signal no matter where in town you are."

"That would be disappointing." He lifted the radio from the dash. Keyed the mic. "This is Deputy Marshal Trent. Is someone there?"

Static was his only reply.

"Something is going on, right?" She gripped the wheel, concentrating on driving in her lane and not freaking out. "I'm not crazy. There's a whole bunch of cartel guys running around these woods all looking for me. And now it's worse."

He sounded like he was talking through gritted teeth when he said, "Now it's worse."

Great. Amy bit her lip and nudged her foot down on the gas pedal. No. That wasn't going to be good. She eased off for the corner, half worried they would come up against some kind of roadblock. A group of cartel members waiting with their weapons, ready to kill her.

But there was no one around the corner.

They saw no cars on the road all the way to town. At the medical center, a single car had been parked at the far end of the parking lot. Amy drove all the way up to the front doors and jumped out.

"I'll carry him. You get them to bring a bed out."

She nodded and ran to the front doors, leaving the driver's door open. She pushed on the door and nearly fell inside. "Help! We need help! The sheriff has been shot!" She didn't know if that was true, but it was probably what'd happened. He could be a deputy.

A nurse ran out, wary-eyed but ready to help. Black scrubs and a short pixie cut. She was probably in her fifties and had the build of a woman who watched what she ate and worked on her feet all day—but still loved to treat herself to dessert. "Where is he?" Amy waved at the door. "We need a gurney, or a stretcher, or whatever it's called."

The woman grabbed a phone from the empty reception desk and hit one button. "Bring a bed." She replaced the receiver.

Amy said, "Is something going on?"

Before the woman could answer, Noah strode in hauling the lawman over his shoulder again.

A male in blue scrubs pushed a bed down the hall. Noah laid the lawman down. "It's just the two of you?"

The woman's full attention was on the man on the bed. "That's Deputy Higgins."

"Let's get him in the back so we can check him out." The man was younger and looked more scared than any of them.

Amy took a step back.

Noah glanced at her. "What is it?"

"They'll take care of him. We should get out of their hair."

Noah looked at the woman. "What's going on?"

She took a step back on her white sneakers. "Everything is fine. She's right, be on your way." The pointed look she gave Noah wasn't lost on Amy. She wanted them gone.

Amy turned to the door. Whatever was happening here, these people would fare a whole lot better if she left. Maybe if she'd never come in the first place that would have been best. But this was where the marshals had placed her. It had seemed like a nice quiet town to put down roots in, so she hadn't objected.

Her eyes filled as she pushed the front door open again.

"Hold up." Noah caught up to her.

She squeezed her eyes shut as he angled her out of the way.

"I go first."

"Right." She tried not to let the conflicting emotions bleed through to her tone but was pretty sure he caught all of it. He could probably read her like no one else ever had.

She'd figured she was keeping her own counsel with her emotions her whole life. But maybe that wasn't true.

Maybe it was just that no one had cared to see what she really felt, below the surface. Until Noah.

He pushed outside and she heard the roar of an engine. Rotors. Amy followed him, wondering if it was state police. Or a TV news station reporting on the prison break, maybe.

Seconds later a helicopter flew overhead.

Time to run again?

Noah reached over and grabbed her hand. "Let's go."

SIX

"Looks like it set down over there." Noah pointed out the windshield, then made a right turn.

"That's the park area out front of city hall."

"If it's clear of trees there's probably enough space to land." He still didn't like this, though. He had no phone signal. No way to tell if the occupants of that helicopter were friend or foe. One meant rescue, the other meant more running.

The marshals, or the cartel?

He turned a corner. On the sidewalk, an older woman wearing warm clothes and white sneakers hustled along. More than a power walk. She glanced behind her, then hurried down the street. Running away.

At the far end of this street, on the corner at the crosswalk, two men stood together in conversation. Both had dark hair and red-tipped ears from the cold. No gloves, black boots. The bottom half of their pant legs were wet.

Men from the woods. Possibly the same ones who had chased them. He didn't know.

Noah kept driving. What else could he do? Then he saw a side street halfway down the block. He tapped the gas and took the turn faster than he should. At the last second he saw the men recognize them.

Noah gripped the wheel.

Amy twisted to look out the back window. "He got his phone out."

"They'll be calling in a sighting of us. Are they following?"

"I don't think so." Her voice still shook. That quaver of fear he didn't like.

It might be realistic to be scared, and he wasn't going to tell her not to be. Still, Noah would rather Amy were somewhere safe by now. Or that she'd never gotten into this situation in the first place.

But that would be impossible. Life was about choices, and she'd done the right thing. It had cost the life of her nephew, but she was moving on. Trying to get free.

He wanted to be there to the end, if he could.

If she would let him be part of the happy ending of her story.

"We need to ditch this car."

Amy said nothing. Noah pulled into someone's driveway. The sheriff's department probably had GPS on all their vehicles. If he and Amy were going to get out of here, then they needed a way to do that without being tracked.

He pulled up the emergency brake and shut the engine off, leaving the keys inside. "Come on."

They hopped out, and he shifted places with her so he could hold her right hand and have his gun in *his* right hand. He wanted her with him. Connected. And he wanted to be able to defend them both.

"Seems weirdly quiet," she commented as they turned onto the sidewalk.

"Empty." No one was outside, apart from that older lady he'd seen running from the two men.

Across the street Noah saw the slats of a blind in someone's front window snap shut. They were being watched? Or whoever it was wanted to make sure they stayed out of sight.

"This feels weird."

Noah squeezed her hand for a second to try and impart some reassurance in her. Hopefully it worked. But until they were actually out of here, neither of them was going to relax.

"It's up here?" He pointed with their joined hands.

Amy nodded. "To the right."

"Okay." He didn't want to go out into a common area if they were going to be exposed, so he slowed at the end of the street.

Then he checked behind them. No one had followed. He crouched and looked around the corner. *Please be the marshals.*

The helicopter rotors had powered down. A group of men milled around. Noah drew his phone and took pictures of them, trying to zoom in far enough to make out...

That was the cartel's number two.

His stomach dropped. "It's not help."

They needed to get out of here, and fast. Too many men. They were outnumbered, and outgunned. Noah would love to arrest that guy right now. Take him in. Get all the respect and accolades for bringing down a key player in the cartel, one they'd never able to pin down. A man on the FBI's Most Wanted list.

Now he was here. Surrounded by foot soldiers all looking for Amy.

"Who is...?"

Behind the cartel number two, another man climbed from the helicopter. Jeremiah Sanders. Amy's brother.

Noah shifted. "We have to go."

The street was still empty. They needed a car. A way out of town.

"What—"

He cut her off. "It's not help. It's more of their guys." He tugged her back down the sidewalk. Should he tell her?

"Noah."

She knew. "Your brother is here." Amy said nothing. "I don't want to be standing around when they spot us."

She nodded, her face flushed. Her hair was disheveled. "Okay."

He picked up the pace and they started to run. But where? Aside from that sheriff's department vehicle, how were they supposed to get out of town to a safe place? He wasn't about to steal someone's car. Help appeared to be limited.

It was like the whole town had been put on lockdown and every resident confined to their homes. Which was good, as it helped them to avoid collateral damage when bullets started flying. Who wanted an innocent caught in the cross fire?

But the eerie quiet was bizarre enough it caused a niggling feeling in him. How were they supposed to get out? Her brother and all his cartel buddies were here. Jeremiah had escaped prison for the express purpose of flushing out Amy so he could get revenge.

Amy squeezed his hand. "Jeremiah is really—"

A man turned the corner at the street where they'd left the car.

"—here?"

There was no time to answer her question. He shoved her across the street. "Go!"

Noah raced with her to the far side of a car parked on the street. She crouched behind it as the first bullet flew at them. Then he crouched and returned fire over the hood of the car.

Jeremiah was here.

Amy resisted the urge to clap her hands over her ears and pretend she was anywhere but here. It might work for a toddler trying to hide from the world, but she was a grown woman.

She slid the gun from the back of her waistband and crawled to the rear of the car. If the gunman came into view, and there was anything she could do, then she would absolutely defend herself. But Noah was a marshal. He was the federal agent here, and she wasn't.

He would probably never forgive her if she put herself in danger.

The man was out of sight. Noah fired again. She heard the cartel guy grunt as one of the bullets Noah had fired struck him. She didn't want to be glad for someone getting hurt, even if it was a criminal, but there was nothing else they could do. These people were trying to kidnap or kill her. Right now they were like a swarm of ants crawling over a summer picnic.

She bit back a whimper and crawled close to Noah. Over his shoulder she saw two men round the corner. "More of them are coming."

He looked. "And they're bringing friends with them."

Amy got ready to run when he told her to. She'd never anticipated wanting to leave this town as badly as she did right now. In fact, she had thought she would live here the rest of her life, hiding from her brother and his friends.

She looked over. Two men ran up behind the first two. They tackled them from behind. Shoved them to the ground and hit them with what she realized were baseball bats. Amy winced. Locals? But whether they were or not, Amy didn't want to hide behind this car forever.

She was exposed in the street. Out here, waiting for some-one to pick her off.

She spun, aiming the gun around her just in case more people ran up from another direction. The two men who had tackled the gunmen advanced on them next. The first one started to close in on her and Noah saw the star badge on his belt.

"Marshal?" The man then eyed her. "Is this business all about you?" Instead of answering him, Noah said, "We need a car." He stood up, keeping her behind him. Making it clear she was under his protection. "Then we'll be on our way, and you can have your town back."

The man eyed him and Amy. "Or we can turn you two over to them and it'll be done a whole lot faster."

She didn't like the sound of that. Nor did she like the look in his eyes. "We're leaving." She put all the confidence and bravery she didn't feel in her voice. It didn't matter what they tried. They weren't the thing she feared.

Jeremiah was here.

She lifted her chin. "We need a car."

"I'll give you a ride," one of the men suggested.

Before she could object to that—no, thank you—Noah did it first. "That's not happening. I don't want more collateral damage than there already has been." He waved at the two men on the ground. Blood had pooled on the sidewalk. Were they dead?

These guys were wild cards. She wouldn't have gone with them even if Noah had agreed to it. "Let's go." She put her hand on his arm.

Noah took a step back, then another. She had to move, as well. The two of them backed away from the men, Amy behind him the whole time.

When they were far enough away, Noah turned. "Come on."

They jogged back toward the sheriff's department vehicle. When they turned the corner and she could see it, Amy breathed a huge sigh of relief.

Noah glanced over. The look on his face was like he wanted to smile, but this wasn't the time. True. But it was nice, even just for a second, to have that shared moment of connection.

He pulled open the driver's door. "They busted out the radio."

She got in on the passenger side and saw the damage. "That isn't all they did."

Wires hung down under the steering wheel.

Noah got in. He selected two and touched them together. Trying to hot-wire it? Whatever he was attempting to do, it didn't work. He sat back in the chair. "We aren't getting out of here in this."

"What are we going to do?"

He looked at his phone. "Still no signal. I'm beginning to think someone's blocking it deliberately."

"Because my brother is here now, and he doesn't want to be found?" She didn't want to see the look in his eyes, so she watched out the front window of the small SUV.

Noah touched the back of her hand, his palm warm. She wanted to shut her eyes, but if she did that she wouldn't be able to see danger coming.

"I'm going to keep you safe, but to do that we need to keep moving."

She nodded and he squeezed her hand. Amy turned to him then. "Thank you for being here."

His eyes softened. "There's no way I'd let you do this alone."

The words warmed her. She felt the corners of her lips curl up as she opened her mouth, ready to tell him he'd been sent here for his job.

The back window of the car shattered. A bullet hit the front window and lodged in the glass, splintering it out in every direction.

If they'd been any closer to each other...

Amy screamed.

SEVEN

Noah reached over and shoved her head down. She was already ducking. He looked at the side mirror, then out the back. Couldn't see anything.

The crack of gunshots continued. A steady stream. Not automatic fire, just relentless. They had to get out of there. But stepping out of the car meant being in the line of fire.

Noah let down the emergency brake. Then he cracked the car door enough to stick his foot out. He twisted and pointed his gun out the space between the frame and the door and fired three shots while he kicked off the ground. They needed momentum. Getting the vehicle moving from a complete stop required a good push, but he got it going.

The small SUV started to roll. Along the street, thankfully slightly downhill. He kicked again to gain some speed. Amy looked up from the passenger seat.

"Stay down until I tell you. Then I want you to get out as fast as you can and run for it." He could cover her. What mattered was that she get away.

She grabbed the door handle but didn't pull it. "What about you?"

"I'm going to be covering you. So when I say, just run.

Okay?" That last part was rhetorical. He wasn't looking for her agreement, and given the look on her face she knew that.

Knew they had limited options.

Knew this was about her being safe and getting away.

Still, she said, "I don't want to get lost."

"I don't want to lose you, either. Especially not when my phone isn't working." He took a breath. "I don't want to get separated."

The car rolled to the cross street. This was going to be fast, and they both had to be prepared to do what they needed to do. As soon as they'd cleared the last house, he said, "Go now."

Amy yanked the door handle and stumbled out of the rolling vehicle.

Noah did the same on his side, already firing as he got out. One perpetrator, end of the street, ducked behind a car.

Noah fired twice. The slide on his gun jammed. He was empty.

The man lifted up and fired. Before Noah could move, fire sliced through the outside of his right arm. He cried out.

The SUV cleared his hip. If he stayed here he was going to get shot, so he raced after her. Noah holstered his gun as he moved, wincing at the burn. He could feel the wet of blood on his arm and the sleeve of his jacket.

He caught up to her partway down the street. "Gun!"

She glanced around wildly, then must have realized what he'd said. He'd love to have explained it to her. Thankfully, she handed over the one she held and he holstered his weapon to be ready to use the other.

If he wasn't careful firing it, he'd run out of bullets with this one, as well.

"This way." Amy headed for another side street. They ducked down it, and he turned as he ran. Looked in all directions. Watched for anyone in pursuit. Whatever the cartel's number two was doing with Jeremiah, Noah was glad he was doing it somewhere else.

The last thing they needed was for her brother to show up now, when they had hardly any ammo, no plan and no backup.

"How far are we going?" Her breath came heavy and she started to slow. "I feel like we're going to be running forever."

"I don't think he followed, but I could be wrong." Noah slowed with her. He rubbed her back, between her shoulder blades. She glanced over, a small smile on her face. Until she saw his arm.

"You've been shot!"

He dropped his good hand and twisted to look at the wound. Okay, that made his head swim. "Right now it's not important. We need to keep moving and keep watch. We have to be careful, but I think we need to get out of town."

"You need to go to the hospital."

Was she going to have another panic attack? They'd dropped the deputy off there. Maybe they could walk that far, and he could get his arm seen to. The nurse had to treat them, despite her obvious fear.

In the meantime he was going to do his best to ignore it. Because what was the point in letting everything slip into defeat? They were down, but they definitely weren't out. Noah wasn't going to quit until they were forced to admit they'd been bested. Not in the sense this was a competition. But he needed to consider the fact Jeremiah had them outmanned and outgunned, and while they weren't going to quit that did mean the possibility they might lose. Big.

"How are we going to get anywhere?" She lifted both arms, then let them fall by her sides. "We can't call for a ride, and we don't have a car."

"For now let's just keep going." The point was to stay alive, and that would only happen if they weren't cornered.

She blew out a breath, but nodded. She took his hand and they speed walked together. Past the houses of people hunkered down. He figured it was like waiting inside for a storm to pass, hoping there was minimal damage.

They had no idea what was going on out here.

"Maybe the sheriff issued a warning. Like an Emergency Alert, or something." Pain let the words slip out, when otherwise they'd have stayed in his head. Just thoughts.

Amy shrugged one shoulder. "Good. I'd hate for someone to get hurt."

"Agreed."

"Oh." She glanced at him. "I didn't mean—"

"I know. It's okay. I'm okay."

She raised one eyebrow.

Noah tugged on her hand. "Come on."

"There."

Amy dragged herself from her thoughts and looked up the street. Across on the other side a man hauled out two suitcases to the open tailgate of his SUV.

When she saw who it was, she pressed her lips together. Noah wanted to ask that guy for help? He probably didn't even remember her, because she'd been the faceless, nameless bookstore employee. But she remembered perfectly the look on his face when he'd been practically yelling at her about why they didn't have the *latest* bestseller. Like the tiny small-town bookstore could stock every book in the world. Just in case he wanted to buy it.

"What?"

Amy didn't even know how to explain it. She settled on saying, "Just don't expect a warm response. You might wanna lead with the gun, follow up with the badge and maybe think about punching him."

Okay, so that wasn't what she thought he should do. But so far, today was shaping up to be pretty bad, and she was scared. Noah had been shot. He had a few bullets, and then they would be defenseless.

The man looked over as they approached. Amy wriggled her hand out of Noah's. She didn't want the marshal to appear soft. Injured, but not a pushover. This guy wasn't the type to think kindness was a good thing.

"I have a question." Noah's voice rang with authority. "Is there a shelter-in-place order in effect?"

"So what if there is?"

There was.

Noah said, "Do you have a phone that works?" He shifted to show the man his badge. "I need to call in."

"What's that got to do with me?"

"If you don't have a phone, I'll need to take your car. If you want to give us a ride that's fine, or I can just commandeer it."

"You guys can't really do that." He stuck his chin out. "And even if you could, I'm not letting you steal my car."

"I'll bring it back. Or the marshals service will pay you for it."

"You think I care about that? You're not taking my car."

Amy glanced behind them, just to make sure no gunmen were going to start shooting at them for about the hundredth time today. "Maybe we could get some medical supplies. Or a washcloth. The marshal has been shot."

Perhaps that would appeal to him. Though Amy doubted it. It occurred to her that maybe going into this assuming the man wouldn't want to help them had been the wrong thing to do. It could have affected his impression of them.

Amy shook off those thoughts. It was what it was. She tried to be positive normally. To see the best in people. But where had that gotten her? She'd had to face the fact her brother was working with a cartel instead of getting a legitimate job to support his son. He'd taken the easy route. The quick payday. She tried to be honest, and where had that gotten her? Doing the right thing brought her here. On the run with a wounded marshal, trying to convince the meanest person in town to help them.

The man shot her a look, like she'd recently crawled out from under a rock and he didn't like the look of her.

Noah said, "We really need your help."

The man turned away. At the last moment she saw the smirk on his face. He reached into the car and came back with a gun.

Amy nearly screamed in frustration. "Seriously? You can't shoot a federal agent! Do you know what the repercussions of doing that are?"

He turned to her. Amy realized she'd said that aloud. She took a step back and lifted her hands. "We're leaving. Try not to shoot a federal agent in the back while we do."

They were just trying to get out of here. Why did this guy have to pull a gun?

The man said, "I'm within my rights to defend my property."

Noah said, "Hold up a second, Amy. This guy is going to put his weapon down. *Then* we're going to leave."

She hadn't figured he would want to turn his back on someone with a gun. Amy moved behind him, but with enough space. Even as she took those couple of steps she felt the heat of anger rise in her.

"You know what?" she yelled at the guy over Noah's shoulder. "You need to back off. We've been shot at. Noah has been *shot*. We have bigger problems right now than you being belligerent. Forget we ever came over here and spoke to you. You're not worth it. But if you cause problems for us—"

"You can take the car." The voice was female.

They all turned. A woman stood at the doorway. Amy expected her to look beaten down, but she didn't. Chin high. Nice outfit, something Amy would have worn to work in an office. She was older than Amy, owning her fifties in a way Amy would like to say she would do when she reached that age.

The woman jingled a set of keys in her hand, then tossed them.

Amy caught the keys.

Belligerent guy turned. "Mandy—"

"They need help." She turned and went back inside. Like that was all she had to say. Like her man wasn't standing in front of them, holding a weapon. She evidently didn't want to wade in, just did what she could to resolve the situation and then bailed.

Amy clicked the locks. A car beeped, but it wasn't the SUV.

A second later the garage door started to roll up. Inside was a sporty full-size car. White, with vanity plates. Evidently the wife, or girlfriend—whatever she was to this guy—was a *sassy gal*. Amy almost smiled.

The man's lips thinned.

She nearly screamed out her frustration this time. Again. She'd lost count. "Are you going to shoot us?"

Even as she asked, Noah ushered her around the back of the SUV. He called out, "If you could *not*, that would be great."

The guy stood there. Held the gun while they pulled out of the drive. Stared at them as they drove away in the woman's car.

Amy shuddered.

EIGHT

"I'd hate to be a fly on the wall when they 'discuss' what just happened in a minute."

Out the corner of his eye, he saw Amy wince. He said, "You mean when they fight about it?"

She clipped her seat belt. "If I'd had my purse, I'd have given him my therapist's card. Seems like they might need someone to talk to." She sighed. "Where to now?"

Noah tapped the steering wheel as they neared the end of the happy couple's street. "Sheriff's office?"

She said nothing, just shifted in her seat.

"I know today hasn't exactly gone as planned, but we have a vehicle again. So we get to a phone and get out of town. Right?"

He didn't want to make a promise he might not be able to keep. Right now he figured she was worried about the fact her brother was here, in town. This had to be about reassurance, not reminding her of the risks. "Jeremiah, or any of those guys, aren't going to get to you. Not if I have anything to do with it. We've fought them off so far, haven't we?"

She nodded.

Noah wanted to squeeze her hand again, but they'd done that a lot so far today. As much as he liked it, what he couldn't do was get too comfortable. Then he'd start assuming more to it than just helping reassure her in that simple way.

Noah didn't need to get used to her being with him, needing his support. Within a day or so—maybe even hours if he just drove straight through to the closest office of the US Marshals—they would go their separate ways. She would be sent somewhere else. He might never see her again.

What would that leave him with? Just the memory of a few stressful hours that only came about because he'd been the closest marshal when the call came in.

Given how he suspected he truly felt about her, he'd probably have a broken heart along with the memories. Not more than that. He certainly wouldn't have her in his life.

Which was exactly the reason he wasn't even going to think about his feelings. Did it matter that he was seriously attracted to her? Nothing could come of it. Never mind how he felt when she looked at him with that trust clear in her gaze. She believed he would take care of her.

The threat was deadly enough that she had to rely on the marshals. She couldn't do this alone, and the one they had sent to deal with it was him.

A fact he thanked God for.

He'd volunteered even before his boss could tell him that he'd assigned Noah to do exactly what he was doing now, because he'd been closest to Amy. Everyone else who could be spared was out in the Northwest looking for the escaped prisoners—one of which was here.

Amy shifted in her seat. "I'd rather get out of town than head for the sheriff's office. Seems to me like just making a run for it will serve us best."

He agreed. "It will give us the least chance of being seen by anyone else around town if we just go."

She shuddered. He caught the tail end of it out the corner of his eye. Noah wanted to pull over and take the time to reassure her, but he couldn't. Not when every time they'd turned around since he'd shown up at her cabin someone had been there, shooting at them. His arm stung, but not as badly as he'd have thought. Only if he moved too far, too fast. Must not be so bad.

Which was good, since he had no opportunity to get stitches right now.

Noah pulled out his phone as he drove the empty streets around the outskirts of town. At least, as far as he could tell, that was where they were headed. Going in the general direction of the highway, with Amy giving him directions.

Noah slowed down and glanced once at the screen, then dropped the phone into the cup holder. Still no signal. Could the cartel really take out a cell tower? Whether they had, or he just had no signal in this town, the result was the same.

They needed to get to a phone.

Maybe at a gas station on the highway. He needed to call the office and inform them what was happening in this town. Tell them to come and round up Jeremiah and all his cartel buddies. Because Noah certainly couldn't do that himself *and* manage to keep Amy safe at the same time.

"So long as Jeremiah doesn't find me." She ran her palms down the legs of her jeans to her knees. A nervous gesture.

There was something she wasn't saying. He knew her, from time spent together during the trial. This was more than just not wanting to face her brother. Amy wasn't hiding something, and he didn't figure she would lie to him. Still...there was something unsaid here.

"Talk to me."

"I'd rather he didn't find me, but that's not only because I don't want to see him. Which, of course, I absolutely do not." She blew out a breath, still doing that nervous gesture.

As much as she didn't want to face it, Noah figured she was terrified. "What is it?"

"I don't want him to find me because of Anthony."

Noah glanced at her for a second, then looked back at the road. "I'm really sorry for what happened to him."

"Uh..." She went quiet for a moment. "You don't know?"

"I don't know what? I heard he was killed in a car accident. Is that not what...oh." The pieces clicked together in his mind. The teen had been a high-value target who'd needed extra protection. Their bad guy a man who would come after his sister for revenge.

To find out what happened to his son.

They could put witnesses who required an additional layer of anonymity in a different kind of witness protection.

The kind where everyone thought they were dead.

"Amy, is your nephew alive?"

Amy blew out a breath. "I have no idea. I mean, the accident was all a fake. But I haven't seen Anthony in a year. He could be anywhere right now, doing anything. In danger. Safe." She lifted her hands, palms up, then let them drop back to her lap. "I have no idea." Noah said nothing.

"You didn't know?"

"I wasn't privy to it." His tone was even.

"Sorry."

He shook his head. "They didn't withhold it for a particular reason. It was just that I had other duties during that time."

"It was pretty early on. After they got to me, and then you guys showed up to save me…" Not a time in her life she was particularly interested in remembering. Those hours she'd been taken were as bad as parts of today had been. But she had to finish her point. "That was the catalyst. Anthony already didn't want to be around me. When the cartel's men got to me, that made it clear we had to make sure they *never* got to him."

"So the marshals faked his death."

"I can't believe they didn't tell you that."

He shrugged then. "I got your full file today. All I did was program your address into my GPS and head out here."

"I'm glad you did."

She was so grateful he'd come. Not just because she had the protection of the marshals service, though that was part of it. But it was so much more. It was the fact that it was Noah.

There was no way she would have wanted to do today with anyone else.

"Haven't you heard from Anthony at all?"

That was a sore subject for her. "No contact."

"I guess that makes it my turn to apologize." He glanced at her. "Sometimes it works out like that. No contact is the safest thing for everyone."

She pictured her nephew in her mind. He would have turned seventeen a couple of months ago. How much had his features changed since she'd seen him last?

She didn't want to remember that final conversation. They hadn't left things in a good place.

Understatement.

"What?"

She bit her lip for a second. "I wanted to go with him. Like, they could put him somewhere safe first and then I could come and live with him later." She took a breath. "He said he'd rather be on his own, or even with a foster family, than ever see me again." It had actually been a whole lot worse than that, but she was paraphrasing. "He told me he hated me for testifying. For what I did to our family. About as much as he hated his father for being a criminal in the first place. He told me he never wanted to see me ever again."

Noah reached over and squeezed her hand. Then he pulled his hand back to the steering wheel.

Amy blinked back the tears that filled her eyes. "I really hope he's okay." She bit the quiver in her lip, then said, "The last time I saw him he was yelling at me." He'd said he hated her. Amy had let him go, knowing the truth was that he would be safer somewhere far from her. Hopefully that had remained true in the year since.

She couldn't think of anything worse than her nephew being on the run, chased by gun-shooting cartel foot soldiers.

Finally, on an open stretch of highway, Amy leaned her head back against the headrest and shut her eyes. Were they free of gunmen following and shooting at them? She wanted to believe she was safe now. That she could trust God to continue to keep them safe—which, of course, she could. He was the same God that He had been yesterday. The same He had been that day Noah and his people had rescued her from that house. And the same God He would be years from now.

A verse she'd read just that morning came back to mind. She believed in Him, with full faith that He would take care of her. *Help my unbelief.* Maybe that might not make sense to some, but to her it was the truth. That push and pull of trust and doubt. An honest explanation of the state of her heart.

"Okay?"

She opened her eyes and glanced over at him. "Yeah."

She was okay. Was she all right? Not really. She wanted… Amy didn't even know what she wanted. Time. Peace. A date with the man she was attracted to.

She blew out a breath.

"Hungry?"

"I could use coffee." She patted her stomach, not entirely sure she could handle a meal right now. Adrenaline had left an unsettled feeling in its wake, along with a drenching fatigue. Like being caught outside in a rainstorm that pounded the earth with big fat droplets of water.

Nothing like the slow float of fat snowflakes now falling.

Noah shifted in the driver's seat. She didn't think much about it, until he adjusted the rearview mirror.

Then he adjusted the side mirrors.

"What is it?" She didn't really want to ask, but what was the point of being naive about the danger she faced? It was her life. Might as well stand and face it. Try to be brave.

"I'm sorry." He sighed. "I'm really sorry. I wanted this to be done. I wanted you to be safe." He sounded quiet. Resigned. Almost defeated.

That was the last thing she wanted. For him to be blaming himself about what was happening. All this was because of her brother.

"I know." It wasn't like she blamed him. He'd been shot, and he'd been a total professional all day. She would probably be dead right now if it hadn't been for Noah. "Just tell me what it is."

"Someone is behind us. I think it's cartel guys in pursuit." He worked his jaw from side to side. "And they're gaining on us."

NINE

Noah glanced at the rearview every minute or so. The truck behind them was picking up speed. It swerved erratically, as though the occupants were on a Friday night joyride through town. Not a hot pursuit to capture Amy. If the cartel succeeded, who knew what would happen to her? One thing was certain—she'd likely wish for death before it came.

Noah gripped the wheel. Determination swelled in him again, rushing up as it clenched his stomach. There was no way he'd let them get her. But could he really keep her out of their hands? Wanting backup to come wasn't going to help. Not if they didn't even know he needed help. And they probably didn't even know Jeremiah was here, in town.

He didn't want to give in to the despair, but his emotional state didn't much count right now. What counted was that they were together and alive. He and Amy both had some fight left in them. Noah would go down swinging, if it came to that.

"What are we going to do?"

Noah heard her breath coming fast. He glanced over quickly, before the bend in the highway. "We're going to press on. Okay?" He didn't wait for her to agree. "This is about keeping you safe. It's about keeping on fighting, regardless of how we feel."

She could have another panic attack. If she did, they would deal.

"Then what should *I* do?"

Noah didn't have an answer to that. "Hang on." That was about the best he could offer her. "I'm going to try and lose them, but they could pursue us until we both run out of gas. Or they could have friends up ahead waiting to block our path."

"Or that helicopter."

That was probably his biggest worry about this whole thing. He couldn't call out. He checked, considering they were farther from town now. Still no signal. When he got to the segment of highway where he'd spoken to his boss earlier, would he have the ability to call out then? Noah wasn't sure.

More worry.

What he didn't want was to be ambushed and over-whelmed. There was no way to fight off a force like that. Not if he wanted to live, and keep Amy from being taken away.

He glanced back again.

The pickup was close now. Tracking with him every time he swerved the car to the side.

Amy was turned around. She watched out the back window. "Do you think that couple told them we were in her car?"

The idea he might've been sold out occurred to him again. "I don't know. I'd wonder if they were tracking my phone if I actually had a signal. There's no way for them to be tracking my GPS when it's not connected to any cell tower or on Wi-Fi." It was half a comment, half a question.

Amy shrugged. "I don't know any of that stuff. Just what I've read in the thriller novels we stock at the store." She winced. "And most of those are pretty scary. I'd hate to think any of that is going to happen to us."

Noah sniffed out. Not a laugh, or anywhere close to it. He didn't have the strength to devote to emotions. Not when he needed all his resolve to hang on to Amy through whatever came.

Should he tell her how he felt? Tell her that this was far more than him being a professional and trying to do the best he could at his job?

He was here because it was Amy. Because she trusted him to protect her. Because she looked at him as though he was the only one who could. Maybe that was all wrapped up in his badge and gun, but he had a niggling feeling she felt something for him. That maybe her feelings matched his, and she wanted it to be him that was here.

She had thanked him. He'd thought, at that moment, maybe…just maybe…she meant *him*. Not the US Marshal Noah. Just Noah.

He adjusted his grip on the wheel. The muscles in his hands were starting to cramp from the tension. "When are they going to make their move? What are they waiting for?"

Amy twisted again. Shifting from looking at the side mirror, to looking out the back window. "I think they're getting closer." She paused. "It's almost like they're herding us."

He glanced in the rearview. "That's what I'm worried about."

There didn't seem to be any way to get off this highway. To take a side road, or different street, and avoid wherever these guys wanted them to end up.

It wouldn't be good, wherever it was. He didn't want to find out what might happen there.

"I need a turnoff." He looked, even though he'd been looking for a couple of miles now.

"What if it's the turn they want you to take?"

That was another problem. He had several right now. Noah blew out a breath and prayed, asking for wisdom to know what to do. His lips moved, the words spilling from his mouth as a whisper.

"Why didn't I think to pray?" Amy shook her head, then her lips moved as she did the same.

He reached over and held her hand. United together here, in the middle of danger, because of their shared faith. The trust they both had that God would continue to safeguard them. That He would bring them out of this.

"Amen."

She squeezed his hand. "Amen."

The pickup truck engine revved. It gained speed. Noah grasped the wheel with two hands just as the other vehicle bumped the back of them.

Amy choked back the scream. She was *not* going to freak out. Not this time, despite how much she wanted to.

The car lurched forward, then swerved. Amy grabbed the door handle and tried not to cry. Or whimper. All those noises she hated to make. No matter how strong she wanted to be, and tried to tell herself she was, they came out, anyway.

They were going to die.

She bit her lip so hard she tasted blood, letting out a moan because of that tiny prick of pain.

Amy twisted again. "They're right behind us."

"I know." He gripped the wheel, the muscles of his

forearms flexing. Any other time she might have been distracted by it.

But not right now.

Amy had to shove all those thoughts out of the way. It had been helpful to think about him before, while they were running for their lives. To distance herself from the fact she'd been about to die. And Noah was a good distraction.

Well, she hadn't died those times. This could be the time, though. The end for her and Noah. She didn't want him to realize he'd failed. Amy didn't like thinking about that. Instead, she decided that keeping Anthony safe, and not letting Noah think he'd done anything wrong, was the important thing.

The pickup behind revved its engine again and slammed into them. Her whole body was jolted forward. Amy nearly hit her face on the dash.

Noah tugged on the steering wheel. The car swerved toward an embankment.

Amy held her breath. Were they going to go over it? Better than a cliff, but she didn't like the idea of bumping over a berm and then having the air bag explode in her face.

He yanked both hands to the left. The traction control light flashed on the dash. She knew what it was because hers used to come on when it was cold in the car she'd had years ago—the one she'd been about to gift to Anthony right before she got involved in Jeremiah's arrest.

Yet another way her "doing the right thing" as everyone called it had ruined more than one life. Or, at least, it had ruined her plans. What she'd thought her life would be. How she'd assumed it would go.

Amy had spent the first few weeks in this town grieving the loss of that promise. The death of all those dreams she'd had. Then she had made new dreams.

Noah hadn't been featured in any of them. A fact she didn't dwell on too much because it was so painful.

He grunted, the tires caught on the road again and the past quit flashing before Amy's eyes.

She blew out a breath. Her hands cramped from holding on for dear life.

The next bump was bigger, making the car sway again as Noah lost control. Her head glanced off the window hard enough that black spots flashed across her vision. Or maybe she just lost awareness as her consciousness blinked in and out.

The car hit the rumble strip at the side of the highway. "No." She didn't want to end up in a ditch.

She heard Noah grunt, and tried to turn to him. The movement of the car jolted her back and forth. The front bumper glanced off a tree. Amy cried out.

Noah's shoulder hit hers.

Amy swayed back toward the window to keep them from banging their heads together. She hit the window again. Brought her hand up and pressed it against the glass.

They hit another tree. The tires skidded on a patch of icy snow and the car started to spin.

It turned a full circle.

The back end clipped a stump, or downed tree, under the snow. The glass of the window shattered under her palm.

She cried out and lowered her hand.

She should have told Noah how she felt. No matter that they couldn't do anything about it. No matter that nothing could, or would, happen between them. That wasn't the point, was it? She should have said the truth out loud, instead of leaving it unspoken for him to maybe wonder. It wouldn't matter if he didn't feel the same way.

She should have told him.

The car high-centered on a mound of snow. The engine revved. Tires spun. Amy's breath was a rush in her head. Each inhale and exhale made the sound fill her ears like a whirlwind. The pumping of her heart was so hard she felt like her chest wasn't big enough to contain the thump.

She looked over. "Noah."

He was slumped over the air bag on his side. She shoved hers out of the way and tried to reach for him. Pain screamed through her arm. She cried out again.

The door beside her opened.

Amy screamed as she twisted to see who it was. Not her brother.

"Shut up." The man cuffed her across the face.

Then she saw the knife. He was going to stab her? But he didn't. It glinted in front of her, and then he slashed the air bag. It deflated. Her arm lay in her lap, feeling funny even though it looked fine. Had she done something to it? The gruff-looking man pulled on her other arm. Pain sparked in her hand, like a hundred tiny needles on her palm. He hauled her out of the car.

"Noah!" She tried to yell as loud as she could, but it was barely audible. He had to wake up. They would kill him and leave him here, and then she would be alone, and—

A thousand thoughts ran through her head. Each breath was like a week, the space between them an entire litany. *Wake up. Wake up. God, help me. Help him.*

"Don't just stand there. Get her legs or something."

She blinked. A second man came into view. That was when she realized she wasn't walking.

They were hauling her away.

TEN

Noah heard something above the rushing in his ears. His entire body felt like he'd been hit by a truck. Or maybe an airplane.

A groan escaped his lips and he pushed off the dash as he sat back. Pain ripped through the outside of his arm. He shoved at the air bag and then shifted so he could get out.

As he grabbed the door handle, what he hadn't comprehended at first occurred to him.

Amy wasn't in the passenger seat.

She was gone.

He stumbled out of the car and had to bite back the groan as he braced his injured arm against the door. The price of staying upright was more pain in his arm. Enough to cloud his vision with moisture. He blinked it back.

He had to get to Amy.

The pickup truck had stopped about fifteen feet back. He trudged through snow, cold wet jeans touching the skin of his lower legs. The discomfort of it was enough to distract him from the pain in his arm.

Noah pulled his weapon. He blinked. Took another step. Should have drawn it before he got out of the car.

But there was no time to berate himself for not thinking straight right now.

They were about to load Amy in that tiny sideways seat in the pickup, behind the passenger seat.

His legs started to numb. His arm hurt badly enough he thought about grabbing a handful of snow and holding it against the graze he'd gotten. Numbness in his arm would feel pretty good right about now.

Both men had their backs to him, struggling to get her to the pickup. Noah probably had two bullets.

He lifted the gun and then angled his steps to the left. Got a clear shot.

Took it.

The other guy spun around. He let go of Amy in the process. She started to fall, squished between the man and the vehicle. The gunman fumbled for his weapon.

Noah ran to him and slammed his gun down on the man's temple. Might as well save the bullet. The man slumped to the ground. Noah relieved him of his gun.

He crouched by Amy. Her eyes were open, but glassy. "Hey." He touched her cheek, swiping his thumb over the flushed soft skin.

She let out a moan that might have been, "Hi," but didn't really sound like anything. He checked the two men weren't going to attack while his attention was on her, stowed his gun and hauled her to her feet. He deposited her on the passenger seat of the pickup.

Her head lolled to one side and she moaned, then drew her arm closer to her. Noah folded her legs in and then shut the door. He could buckle the seat belt when he got in.

He stowed his gun in its holster, and then tucked the gunman's weapon in the back of his jeans.

Noah pressed the palm of his hand—of his good

arm—against the door of the pickup and just took a minute. Pain from aches and bruises sparked as he inhaled, and then pushed out the breath. *Thank You, God.* He'd gotten her back because God had protected them.

The way He'd done a thousand times already today.

Noah was pretty sure this was going to shape up to be the longest day of his life. He rounded the truck to the driver's door and saw that—*thank You, God*—they'd left the keys in the ignition.

This town was so isolated it would take them an hour to get to a gas station. Amy could be in a major medical crisis.

He had to turn back to the medical center.

Even as he thought through it, Noah tapped the wheel with his index finger. His phone still had no signal. He couldn't call out.

Before he drove, he went to the unconscious man and searched his pockets for a cell phone. Or a radio. He had to have some way to get orders from Jeremiah, and the cartel boss that was here, as well as report in.

Why hadn't he thought of that before he got in the car?

Noah didn't have time to think about the implications of the fact he'd probably hit his head.

The man moaned. Noah stumbled back and fell in the snow, but the man didn't wake up. Noah put a hand to his chest and exhaled. No one had seen that. No one knew that he'd been startled enough to fall backward.

He clambered to his feet and winced. Flipped the man over and found a radio in the back pocket. He checked it as he walked back to the driver's side, watching for any more gunmen. Just the crackle of static.

He shut the door. Wondered again about going back to town, versus making a run for it. Stay, and hopefully catch Jeremiah. Go, and keep Amy safe. Could he do both?

Noah looked down at the dash while the engine chugged. Less than a quarter tank of gas. *I guess that's the answer, Lord.* There wasn't enough gas to get to the closest place to fill up, heading out of town. Was there enough to get back to the medical center? Maybe.

He pulled out onto the highway and flipped a U-turn. When they got there, he would use a landline or a computer to get the word out to the marshals.

Maybe they were already on their way.

Noah decided to think the best of it. Amy would be safe. She could get medical attention. He could contact his boss, and get backup here to help take down this army of gunmen.

One he was driving back into the heart of.

God, help us.

Amy blinked. Fluorescent lights overhead flashed behind her eyelids. She blinked again. Shifted. She was on a bed.

The warm tug of something in her arm. She focused on the sensation. Looked at the needle sticking out of the inside of her elbow. *Huh.* Then she lifted her other arm.

Bandaged. A splint.

Someone moved beside the bed. "What…?"

Noah shifted. He sat on the edge of the bed, wearing jeans and a T-shirt. His right arm was in a sling. "Hey. You're awake."

"How long was I out?"

"Maybe an hour, or so. You broke your arm."

"I think I came to at one point." Maybe that didn't matter.

He nodded, though there was no reassurance in his

gaze. They weren't safe. "They think you hit your head, as well. You might have a concussion, but they want to see how you are and then they'll run some tests." He hesitated. "They said in a few days you can get a permanent cast until your arm heals."

She stared at him. "What else?"

"I called my office. They're sending backup."

"Okay." That wasn't it. At least, she didn't think so. Something was wrong, and Noah didn't want to tell her what it was. "I'm a big girl. I can handle it."

He sighed, his lips curling into a small smile. "I know you can." He paused. "The fact is, I don't want you to have to handle it." What did that mean? "I want you to have a peaceful life. A good life, where you're not running for your life." He rubbed at his forehead with the heel of his palm, then ran his hand back through his hair. Disheveled was a good look for him, even though the reason behind it wasn't good.

His shoulders slumped.

Amy reached up with her free hand and touched his cheek. "Noah."

His chocolate-brown eyes glinted, like flecks of gold. Warmth, despite the tension in him. He hadn't relaxed. And it seemed like he wasn't going to.

"What is it?"

"I'm just nervous. And I probably will be until the marshals roll in, along with the FBI and Colorado state police. I told them to bring everyone." A small smile curled his lips. "I'm expecting an invasion anytime now, and hopefully it will be the good guys."

She nodded. Pain thronged through her skull, like an orchestra at the climax of the piece they were playing. She blew out a breath. "I hope so, too."

"I can tell the nurse if you need more pain medicine."

Amy laid her hand on his. "In a minute."

"Don't be stubborn. If you need medicine, you should take some."

She pressed her lips together. But she wasn't mad. They twisted into a smile.

He grinned back. "You're going to make me work for this, aren't you?"

"No way."

It slipped out before she'd even thought it through, the realization that anything personal between them should be the easiest thing in the world. Maybe work would come later. But sharing their feelings for each other?

"I'm glad you're here."

He said, "It's been mentioned. And for the record, I'm glad I'm here, too."

"Really glad."

"Will you still say if Jeremiah finds out you're here, and shows up before the marshals do?" He even looked at his watch.

"Yes. Even if."

"There you go, being stubborn again."

She wasn't going to apologize for that. "I only have a limited amount of time before you leave. I need to make the most of it."

"Before I leave?"

"Or I do. Whatever." Were they going to argue about that? "No more talking."

"And what, pray tell, should we do instead?"

She grabbed a handful of the front of his shirt and tugged on it. "Maybe you should come here and find out."

Noah's lips spread in a smile. He planted his good hand beside the pillow and leaned down, less by her tugging and more by his own volition. He didn't need her to twist his arm. Seemed like he was all in.

But he didn't kiss her.

Noah paused, his face close to hers. "Are we going to do this?"

"I'm done thinking about all the reasons why it was a bad idea before. Because I'm ninety percent sure they're still valid." She searched his gaze with hers. "But what if we never get another chance?"

Things were going to turn out the way God had planned, and they didn't know what that would be. She could only trust that they'd be alive. That the best would happen. But maybe that was an impossible dream, one she wasn't going to receive.

Noah touched his lips to hers. Tentative at first, then it was like he made the decision. Or gave in to the pull of the feelings that seemed to arc between them like sparks of electricity.

Amy forgot everything, and just lived in the moment. Maybe she would regret it later, but the truth was that life really was too short. Who knew what would happen? She wanted to grab a moment of happiness in the middle of all the crazy.

Was that too much to ask?

The door opened.

Noah pulled back, twisting to see who it was. She looked past him and saw the nurse they'd left the deputy sheriff with standing there. The look on her face was shell-shocked. There was no other way to describe it.

"What is it?" Noah's voice rang in the small room.

"They're coming here." Her lip quivered. "I'm sorry. They said they'd kill all of us if we didn't tell them if you showed up again."

And they'd waited this long? Now she was warning them, to give them time to…what? Escape?

Amy shoved at the covers. "Get this needle out of me."

Pain tore through her arm.

"You can't move when that's in!" The nurse rushed over. "Wait…that's actually a good idea. I'm going to tell them that. They can't take you out of here."

"He'll just shoot me right here in this bed."

The nurse gasped and turned to Noah. "You should go. I'll hold them off."

"Not happening." He didn't even move off the bed.

"She's right," Amy said. "You should get somewhere safe. Wait for reinforcements, and then take Jeremiah and his friends down." She patted his arm, half trying to reassure him it was okay and half trying to get him to move away from her. As though that would keep him safe.

Noah turned to her, the look in his eyes like fire. "Not. Happening."

ELEVEN

Noah lowered the radio he'd taken from those men, right before he took their pickup. "They have the whole building surrounded, and it sounds like they're bringing more men in by the minute."

Determined to root out Amy.

He gritted his back teeth together and tried to not let her know that he was scared. For her. For him. For what might happen. For anyone who was here that might get caught in the cross fire. There were so many things to worry about it was beyond overwhelming. *God, help us get through this. Help me figure out how to help her.*

Noah needed serious help. Otherwise there would be multiple casualties, and Amy would be gone.

"What can we do?" Amy glanced from the nurse to him.

Noah didn't have much he could tell her. But he hadn't sat around while they checked her out and put the IV in. They'd stitched up his arm, and insisted he wear the sling. He'd mostly worn it just so when Amy woke up she'd know he had been taken care of. The headache would go away on its own. Hers was probably much worse.

He said, "I put a call out to the marshals service when we got here, remember? Help is on its way." That reminder was the good news. Now for the bad news. "Problem is, your brother and his friends are going to come in here before the good guys even show up. We don't have enough time to wait."

Which meant she could be dead before help arrived. Noah could be dead by then. The damage could already be done, and there would be nothing either of them would be able to do about it.

No way to save her.

"So we should try to get out." She glanced to the nurse again, then back to Noah. "Maybe there's a side entrance we can slip through, get away."

The last thing Noah wanted to do right now was rip this sling off and run. Neither of them were in any state to try to flee again. Though he would if it was their only option. He fingered the radio, not wanting to listen again at how they were surrounding the building. Waiting for the "boss" to show up at the medical center so they could come in and get Amy.

Was Jeremiah the boss? The US Marshals hadn't thought so through the trial. Neither had the Department of Justice, or the FBI. None of the evidence seemed to point to that. Still, it was possible they'd just missed it. Or things had changed since he had gone to jail. Like a favor done, and the return was that he had been given an elevated position. That was essentially speculation, though, and not much more than that unless he could get actual evidence.

"Obviously the best option is for me to just go out there and give myself up." Amy shifted on the bed, shoved the covers back and sat up. She might sound brave right now, but he could see the fear in her eyes. She said, "Jeremiah will stand down if I go to him."

There was no way he'd let her sacrifice herself.

Noah shot her a look. "Really? You know that, do you?" Maybe her brother wanted maximum damage.

She ignored him and asked the nurse, "Get this out, will you?"

The nurse looked at him—the badge in the room, therefore the voice of reason.

Amy said, "He doesn't need to give you permission. Get this thing out of me." She started to tug on it.

"Okay, okay." The nurse practically slapped her hands away. "Don't hurt yourself. Let me do it."

"I'm trying to save all of you." Amy winced. The needle slid all the way out, and the nurse covered the skin with a square of gauze. "Who cares about a little blood?"

Noah did. He really cared about Amy not bleeding. He'd rather she was healthy. Safe.

Was she really going to do this? She seemed determined, but that was going to hit a wall any second now when she realized he wasn't going to let her sacrifice herself. Being noble didn't make it the right choice.

He turned to the nurse. "How many patients do you have right now? How many people in the building?"

"Three, including Amy. Not including you. Six total."

He nodded. Then he turned to Amy. Chin up, that determined look in her eyes.

It very much seemed like she would give herself up to her brother. If he let her.

"You get that my job is to keep you safe, right? The whole point of you being in Witness Security is to make sure of that. That means not letting you turn yourself over to the man who wants to kill you." Noah folded his arms. "The two of you need a place to hide."

The nurse turned to him. "There's—"

A voice came over the announcement speakers. "Clare."

There was a pause. The nurse glanced at a speaker, high on the wall. The way a person turned their attention to a phone call they were on.

"Hopefully you can hear me," the man said through the crackle of the speakers. "I'm not sure if you can, but the deputy they brought in is awake."

"That's good, right?" Amy hopped off the bed like they were too distracted to notice her essentially trying to escape.

Noah said, "Hold up." He lifted a hand, palm out. Just so she would know he was serious. "You're going to find somewhere to hole up while I talk to him." Hopefully that would buy some time, so he could convince her to stick around. "There are people here, and we need to make sure they'll be all right before you do…whatever you're going to do."

Let her think he was going to allow it. The truth would win out. Noah would figure out a way to keep her safe, hopefully with the deputy's help.

He had limited ammo. Limited options.

There was an army outside the door.

"Just give me a little time, okay?"

Amy clearly didn't like it, but he saw her nod.

After Noah had a quiet conversation with the nurse—one she wasn't privy to—Amy and the other woman were ushered to a room. Noah shut the door.

She half expected a lock to turn. Why was he acting like this? She'd had a good idea. He might not like it. Truth was, she didn't much like it, either. It wasn't like she was all fired up to go see her brother. To be killed, or whatever those cartel friends of his were going to do to her, all to shut her up as revenge for testifying. And for costing Jeremiah his son.

Amy shut her eyes. Tried to figure a better way out of this. Of course she would go for another option, but what was there that she could do?

She squeezed the bridge of her nose with her good hand and tried to think. The other arm was basically useless.

"You okay?"

Amy turned to the nurse, who had for some reason been closeted in here with her. "Fine." She didn't want a stranger to get hurt for her.

"Nothing residual from the crash?"

Amy didn't want to shake her head. Her thoughts were a little…swimmy. Like shaking her head would make everything swish around, and she'd get dizzy. "I'm okay." With a list of qualifiers she didn't intend to share.

No jumping. No running. No turning around too fast. No movement at all that was too fast. So long as she stuck to things not on the list, she figured she could convince them she was all right. Or, at least, well enough to be making a decision rationally.

She wandered around the small space. It had a kitchenette. Tiny round table and four chairs. A beat-up love seat. Amy pulled the fridge door open and stared at the contents inside. What else was she supposed to do when confronted with a fridge?

"Hungry?"

Amy shut the door and moved on, around the room. Looking at what was here. "What's been happening in town? We were running through the woods, so we don't really know what has gone on."

"Gunmen rolled in. I saw at least four pickup trucks. Guys in front, and more in back. It was like being in Afghanistan."

Amy lifted her brows. "You served?"

"Medical mission trip. They used to sweep into town, wave their guns around and threaten to kill us if we didn't treat whoever they had with them that had been shot." The nurse made a face. "Mostly I figured it was one of our guys who tried to kill one on their side. So why was I going to help save him? But it's what I signed up to do."

Amy saw her anew through the lens of this information. Maybe if she'd stayed in town, they would have become friends.

Right now she had no idea if she would even live out the rest of the night.

The nurse shrugged. "These guys seemed kind of similar. But without the wounded to treat."

"That would be my fault."

"They're really here for you?"

Amy nodded, small and slow but enough. "My brother is one of those guys who escaped from that federal prison. He brought them here to get me."

Her eyes widened. "They locked down the town. No one is allowed to go anywhere until they find you."

"What about the sheriff—is he doing something?"

The nurse shrugged. "I have no idea where he is, but I wouldn't want to be him right about now. Faced with an army. One of his guys in here. Maybe he's dead."

"Backup is on the way." Great, now she was flinging around the party line. Saying what Noah had said, just because it sounded reassuring. Not because it was actually going to help them get away.

She wandered to the high window, just so she didn't have to see the disbelief on the nurse's face. Neither of them was dumb. There was no way backup would get here in time. Noah had said that. And yet, here they were. Waiting.

Did she want to do this? Not especially.

Was it the right thing? Yes.

Amy did the right thing. That was how she'd decided to define her life. When everything with her brother became clear, and she realized he worked for a cartel, she'd decided this. Maybe even before then. When Anthony had been born she'd been his primary caretaker, even though Jeremiah didn't see that. He didn't even thank her. Or help out with groceries, since teenage boys consumed more food than a small country.

His mother certainly hadn't stuck around. She'd been gone since before Anthony's third birthday. After that Amy did all those "mom" things, taking care of him as much as she could. Being there for him. He hadn't turned out perfectly. Who did? But he was a good kid. Just a little…wild.

And convinced she'd betrayed him, the same way she'd apparently betrayed her brother. According to them. But her beliefs called her to stand for truth. To do the right thing, even if it cost her everything.

Which it had.

Though if she'd kept her head down and never testified, then she would never have met Noah. They'd never have had that…moment. What a tragedy that would've been. She'd take the good with the bad any day, even though the bad had been so hard. Still was. Not much she could do about that.

"I should go and see if Noah and the deputy are done talking."

Maybe they would make a plan. Maybe it would be good, and it would work. This, however, would be much more efficient.

No loss of life.

Except hers.

"I don't think you should—"

Amy hadn't lied yet, and she wasn't going to start doing it now. "It's okay." She held the nurse's gaze for a second, not sure what else to say that wasn't going to make it completely obvious what she was about to do.

The nurse started to object.

Amy strode into the hall, right into view of the front doors. She heard a shuffle behind her, but kept going. Walking fast made her arm hurt.

The nurse yelled, "Deputy Marshal Trent!"

Amy ran for the front door, shoved at the handle and was hit by a wall of cold January air. And a man.

She collided with his chest. Looked up at his face, and swallowed a gasp.

Her brother.

TWELVE

Noah ran into the hallway as soon as he heard the shout. The front door swung shut. She'd done it. She was outside, in the clutches of men who wanted to kill her.

He turned back to the deputy, who was already climbing out of the bed. He started to ask the guy if he had command of everything they'd just discussed.

Before he could say anything, the deputy waved him off. "Go. I've got this."

Noah didn't like it. The guy was seriously pale, and probably shouldn't even be out of bed. He'd have disagreed if he had any other option. Or if he wouldn't have said and done exactly the same thing.

There was no time.

No other way.

Noah ran to the front doors and shoved his way outside. The group was over by a collection of vehicles that had probably shown up like a convoy. Several turned when they heard his approach. He didn't pull his own weapon, considering the lack of bullets. The cartel guy's gun he'd left with the sheriff's deputy so the man wasn't unarmed.

Amy.

She looked over from beside a car, sandwiched between the frame and her brother. As though he was just about to shove her inside.

Noah picked up speed and barreled right toward them. He wasn't exactly sure what he would do when he reached her brother. What mattered was that he did everything he could.

Two men came up from the sides. Noah collided with both, going down in a tangle of grunts and limbs. A gun barrel glanced off his ribs. Pain screamed through his arm where he'd been grazed and stitched.

Amy screamed.

Noah fought as hard as he could with one good arm and—what amounted to—a half. That was about all he had to draw on. Brute force and cunning. The will to do his job and protect Amy. These guys were wily, though. They fought dirty.

One kicked Noah's thigh. White-hot pain sparked and his entire leg numbed like a flash—a light being switched off.

He cried out.

"No!" Amy yelled.

Would she have screamed his name? Had she started, then made it come out as, "No," so her brother never realized who he was to her? That there was something between them. That they cared for each other.

He wanted to believe that. Tried to, even while the blows rained down on him. Kicks. Punches. He grabbed a boot and tossed the guy back. He just hopped a couple of steps, then slammed that same boot into Noah's arm.

He cried out again. Right on his wound. The guy couldn't have landed that more perfectly if he'd known exactly where the stitches were.

He gritted his teeth. Tasted blood in his mouth. Gasped a couple of breaths and tried to get a handle on what was happening. Overpowered. But he wasn't out, despite being down for the count.

"Stop it!" Amy's voice rang in his ears. High. Desperate. He'd never intended her to sound like that. To feel all those emotions for him so strongly she screamed with it.

Noah should never have let her fall for him.

His emotions were what they were, and he wasn't going to allow himself to regret kissing her. Today or the moment when they'd almost kissed a year ago. Both had been the best days of his life. Despite the rest of it. Or maybe especially because of the time spent together, considering the affection was like a flash of warmth in the middle of the worst storm.

"Enough."

The men backed off. Noah didn't move. He just lay there on the frozen concrete and waited.

One of the men said, "Want me to kill him?"

The cartel wouldn't care that he was a marshal. In fact, that might make them more inclined to kill him. He would be a trophy. A prize worth boasting about. Killing a marshal just for sport.

Either way, he'd done everything he could. The deputy would take point when the marshals and whoever else showed up. They would come and find Noah, and Amy. Or what was left of them. It was all a waiting game until then. Buying time and trying to stay alive.

He heard Amy whimper, but didn't look at her. He couldn't meet her gaze or he would probably lose it, as well. The last thing he needed was for these guys to see him cry over her.

"Bring him with us."

Noah's entire body hurt. They hauled him to his feet and he could barely stand. He locked his knees. Tasted

blood in his mouth. He was pretty sure his nose was drip-
ping blood, too.

He locked gazes with Amy then. Saw the tear roll
down her face. Noah wanted to reassure her, to tell her
that everything was going to be fine. Instead, he was
shoved toward a different truck.

He watched her forced into a car by her brother, who
got in the back with her. What would he say to her? Noah
wouldn't know until they got where they were going. He
had to pray they would be taken to the same place. That
he wouldn't just be driven out into the snow in the middle
of nowhere and left to die in the dark and cold of tonight.

Fear was like the wind, rolling in and touching everything as it moved on its journey. Leaving nothing
unaffected.

Noah stumbled. No one caught him.

"Move."

They took him to an SUV and shoved him toward the
open back door. One of the men laughed. Noah tried to
look at him, but his vision got all blurry.

At the last second he was struck from behind. Black-
ness rushed up from the ground to swallow him in a
blanket of unconsciousness. At least there wasn't any
pain.

Amy hadn't realized how much her brother would remind her of Anthony. The loss of her nephew from her
life hurt. Probably more than anything else she'd suffered.

Jeremiah thought he was dead.

Anthony was a vulnerability for all of them. A good
part of the reason Jeremiah had come after her. Her reason for testifying, even if her nephew hadn't agreed. A
minor under the protection of Witness Security. While

she was here, forced to face down her brother. Exactly the way it should be.

So why did she feel like this?

She glanced over her shoulder at those men loading Noah into their vehicle. "What are they going to do with him?"

Fear for Anthony had rolled through her. Now she was full of fear for Noah, as well.

Jeremiah shifted in his seat. "You don't need to worry about that, considering what's going to happen to you." His voice was like road rash. Like scraping your skin on gravel.

If he thought she was going down without a fight, he was going to be sorry. Amy might have tried to give herself up to save everyone else, but that didn't mean standing down. Noah clearly hadn't agreed with her. But what else could she have done?

She studied her brother's profile as the guy in the front seat drove. She would like to have said that he was so different now from the brother she'd known, but Amy didn't think that was true. He'd always had that hard edge to him. A slice of something wild.

"I don't care what you do to me." She spoke to his profile. "But I don't want you to hurt Noah. He's a marshal. It's only going to bring down a world of hurt on you and your associates."

The man in the passenger seat, one of the cartel guys, twisted around. "You think we care he's a fed? We kill guys like him just for fun."

She kept her attention on Jeremiah and watched for his reaction. Maybe it was fruitless to expect something from him. That after all he'd done, there might be a shred of humanity inside him. But no.

His gaze caught the passenger's and she saw the curl

of his lips. Her brother didn't care at all. He would have Noah killed, and he wouldn't care at all.

"That's it?" She didn't know what she was expecting, but the words came out, anyway. "After everything you've done, you're not even going to apologize. You're just going to ruin my life *again*?"

"Ruin *your* life?" The words were snarled at her. A flash of white teeth in the dark of the car. "You're the one who put me in prison."

"Because you broke the law, and you were going to destroy your family."

"Anthony is dead because of *you*."

In a way, Amy figured, that was true. On paper, Anthony was dead. Because of her? Yes, because she'd taken the necessary steps to adequately protect him from his father. By having them declare his son dead.

"You think I don't wish I'd gone with him?"

He scoffed. "You should have."

Then they would both be "dead." At least as far as Jeremiah was concerned. They might be talking about two different sets of circumstances, but they were on the same page. She would rather be with Anthony than here with his father.

Though only as long as she could also still see Noah. *God.* She wanted to cry out to her Father in Heaven. To finally admit the truth. She didn't want this life. She wanted to live a life where she had Noah *and* Anthony, but she'd been too scared to ask for it. Until now. There was nothing else for her to lose. Finally she had nothing but God's will. And she was going to ask for everything. Her nephew. The man she loved.

She wanted all of it.

For too long she'd been scared to ask, for fear it wouldn't be His will for her to have all the things she wanted.

I'm asking now. Please help me get out of this. Save Noah. Help me fix things with Anthony.

She'd been living half a life for so long. Scared. Alone. Getting by with the bare minimum. No roots. No relationships. Now she knew what she wanted, and there was nothing to lose by asking.

"What's done is done." She lifted her chin. "If I die, then I'll do it knowing I did the right thing for my family."

"You killed my son."

It hurt to hear those words. To know her brother believed them. Part of her still loved him. She probably always would, considering he was her brother.

The car pulled up at an out-of-the-way house. Ranch and barn. Additional structures. Too many people, pretty much all of them armed. Like walking onto an enemy base.

Jeremiah got out. Then he leaned in, grabbed her arm and dragged her from the car.

"You're really going to do this."

"You're the one who did *this*." He walked her toward the barn. "Just remember that."

She nearly stumbled. Maybe she should kick and scream. But what was the point? They were going to kill her no matter what.

She spun around, her heart winning out over everything else. She screamed, "Noah!" as loud as she could.

Jeremiah shoved her inside the barn. He shut the door and she had to listen to his laughter as he moved away and she just stood there in the dark.

Listening for the gunshot that meant the end of Noah's life.

THIRTEEN

He'd heard her scream. The sound clenched his heart, right before it tore at it. Threatened to break it right down the middle. *Amy.* He wanted to squeeze his eyes shut and fight off the tears for her. Noah couldn't. Men like these didn't understand emotion. And they for sure didn't understand weakness like that.

They felt nothing.

It was kill or be killed in this world. And Jeremiah Sanders was not the king. That was clear enough when he turned from the barn door and walked to the suited cartel number two. Received his orders. Looked at Noah.

He stood his ground, unflinching under Jeremiah's and his boss's stares. Who cared what they thought? Or what they were going to do with him. Noah needed Amy to live until the marshals showed up. That was all.

How long would it be?

He couldn't think about that. It would lead to a spiral that would suck him down into a depression. His feelings for her never realized. What could be would never come to fruition.

No. It was best to simply hope for the next five minutes. Thirty minutes. An hour.

Beyond that, it was up to God.

Please.

The cartel number two said something. Jeremiah's eyes narrowed. A quick nod, then he walked to Noah and spoke to the man beside him. "Take him out back. Get rid of everything."

"Copy that." The man's voice was like gravel crunched under tires. He jabbed the barrel of a gun into Noah's kidney. "Move."

Noah started walking.

He glanced over his shoulder in time to see the cartel number two call Jeremiah back over. They had some kind of business, probably involving Amy. Noah was just in the way—the fed they needed to get rid of quickly so they could get this done.

There were at least twelve foot soldiers that he could see. Hopefully the marshals would bring more men than that. Between an escaped federal prisoner and the possibility of apprehending one of the FBI's most wanted—the number two cartel boss—he figured they would bring an army.

Don't let her get caught in the cross fire, Lord. Protect her. Protect me.

Give us a future.

The barrel jabbed him again. "Left."

Noah rounded the building. He walked out back to his death, his teeth gritted. The second he could make a move, he was going to. He couldn't fight an army, but he could start with this guy.

Should've tied me up.

They thought they had the upper hand, because they had weapons and he didn't. Noah took a couple more steps. Scanned the area.

No one was around.

He feinted right, shifted left. Dipped his head at the

same time he turned. Probably looked like a great dance move, but there was no time to consider that now. He shoved the barrel of the rifle aside with the flat of his hand and tackled the guy.

He could pick the whole thing apart when he reenacted it for Amy's amusement. Because they'd be laughing about this later, right?

Ouch.

Enough trying to distract himself. They landed on the ground, the gunman on his back. Noah used the momentum to shove the rifle up far enough to hit the guy in the face with it.

Out cold.

Noah grabbed the gun and stood. Checked it. Blew out a breath. Adrenaline spiked in his blood, making his head swim and dulling the pain in his arm. He would pay for it later, but right now all the pain was pushed aside in favor of going after Amy. His job was to protect her, and that was exactly what he was going to do.

Two short high notes of a whistle sounded from the trees. Noah turned. The sight of armed, uniformed men emerging made him lower the barrel of the rifle.

He tried to pick out men he recognized, or someone in charge. They just kept coming. And coming. Armed men. SWAT gear. State police guys in uniform, vests on. All of them were out of breath.

Finally he saw someone he knew. "Withers."

His boss lifted his chin. "This is Lieutenant Barnes."

Noah nodded. "How did you know where we were?"

"Confluence of so many heat signatures," Barnes said. "Got your witness?"

That stung. No, he didn't have her. Not yet, anyway. Noah had to point to the barn. "In there."

The first man lifted two fingers and motioned them forward, each one staying out of sight of the gunmen.

Guess it's go-time, then.

Noah needed to get Amy back. That was his priority. The rest of them could deal with the cartel's army.

He let the SWAT guys—probably FBI armed response—go first. After all, they wore helmets and protective gear he didn't have, and suspect takedown was their job.

Noah watched as they engaged the cartel guys, staying out of sight. He had his shoulder against the barn wall. The same building Amy was in. He looked for a window.

A back door? He needed a way inside that didn't put him in the line of fire trying to get to her through the front. He didn't care about getting injured, but he also couldn't save her if he was dead.

Someone yelled. The sound was muffled. Coming from inside the barn? He fast walked to the front corner and looked out. A full-fledged battle was taking place. Could he get to the front door, where Jeremiah had shoved his sister inside, without being shot?

Noah gritted his teeth and ran for the door. It was open enough for him to slide through, but inside was empty.

Where was she?

Amy winced. "Let go."

Jeremiah didn't. He just kept dragging her. And why? There were gunmen everywhere. "Hurry up."

She tried to keep up. Where were they going, anyway? He dragged her down a path. Her feet were soaked. The snow lay thick and heavy—like the clouds overhead. It was for sure going to dump a load of fresh powder tonight.

Which might have been nice if she'd been inside and

able to appreciate it, instead of being dragged through the snow. She let out a heavy breath.

Her brother said, "Come on. Move."

Who did he think he—

A single man stepped out onto the path in front of them. He lifted a gun and pointed it at her brother. "Think you can simply leave and I'll forget?"

Jeremiah held his body so tight she thought he might snap. Amy huddled behind him. But if her brother was going to get shot, then that probably wasn't the best place to hide. She moved out from behind him.

The cartel guy didn't seem surprised.

Jeremiah shifted. "I was coming to find you."

"No. You were running." He paused. "Take your sister, take my money and disappear?"

"I'm gonna kill her!"

Amy took a step back. He didn't want anyone else to do it. Her brother still hated her, and he was determined to kill her himself.

"And my money?" cartel guy asked.

Amy thought about making a run for it. Just dashing off into the snowdrifts and fleeing for her life. Would she get more than two steps before they shot her in the back?

"She has it." Jeremiah motioned to her.

Amy gaped. "I…what?"

Then it registered that she'd heard a tone in his voice. Her brother was stalling for some reason. To stay alive? To kill her? To get away from the cops?

Jeremiah lifted his chin. "You'll have to take both of us if you want to get it back." He shifted his feet. Nervous. Cold. Playing a game that he wasn't sure he would win.

Amy took a step back.

The gun moved to her. Cartel guy's eyes narrowed.

"I'm not entirely sure about that." He shifted the weapon and pulled the trigger.

The flash of light blinded her for a second. And the sound. A boom that echoed, the noise causing snow to fall from nearby branches, dislodged by the sound.

Her brother's body jerked and he fell.

Amy screamed. Cartel guy grabbed her wrist. "Move it. Or you get shot next." He blew out a breath.

She stumbled trying to keep up. Then looked around. Had anybody heard that shot?

He jerked on her wrist. "I don't have to kill you." He pointed the gun at her shoulder as they walked, him halfway supporting her weight against his. "I could cause you a lot of pain. You'll tell me what I want to know."

She shifted away from his body, not wanting to be anywhere near him. She should tell him she didn't know anything about the money. *No.* If he knew she had nothing to give him, he would simply kill her right here.

Money.

That was what this whole thing was about?

Where is the money?

That was what they'd asked when they'd abducted her before. The marshals had never been able to figure out what they were talking about.

Jeremiah had leveraged their desire to recoup what had been lost into a plot that would leave her dead. An army coming for her. Revenge. Then what would he have done? Killed her, and disappeared?

Her brother was insane.

Or he had been. Now he was dead. All those plans came to nothing now. He'd had no idea his son was still alive.

A tear rolled down her face, though she wasn't entirely sure what she was crying for.

The cartel guy walked her down a snowed-over path until she saw a vehicle, maybe a quarter mile away.

She couldn't let him get her in that car.

Amy started to pull against his grip on her. "Let me go."

He let out a chuckle, a single exhale. Not wasting the energy to actually laugh.

What could she do…?

"Freeze!"

"US Marshals!"

"Put the gun down!"

Amy jerked to a stop. She was so surprised she lifted her hands. Someone grabbed her arm from the right and tugged her away from the cartel guy. Too fast for him to try and reach for her. To make her his hostage, held at gunpoint.

"Put it—"

Shots rang out.

She tried to turn to see, and then she was in Noah's arms. Face pressed against the open collar of his jacket. "Don't look."

She squeezed her eyes shut. He was right, that wouldn't have been good and she really didn't want to see it.

Amy sucked in a full breath and then let it out. It broke a couple of times in the middle, and she whimpered.

His hand shifted, up and down her back. Strength holding her to him. Reassuring her. But Amy needed more than a hug. She shifted her arms and lifted them between her and Noah, to touch the sides of his face. Her bandaged, splinted arm was awkward. She ignored it and lifted her heels at the same time, going up on the balls of her feet.

She pressed her lips to his. Relieved, desperate to process the fact she was safe. They were both alive. She felt him smile, and he returned the kiss. Pulled her close in his arms.

Someone whistled.

Amy pulled back, letting out a small giggle. More relief than humor. They were okay. The cold rushed in, but there in his arms she was warm for the first time in a very long time.

"I love you." The skin of his brows shifted. As though he wasn't sure how she was going to react. There was nothing Amy wanted more than to reassure him.

To tell him that she felt exactly the same way. She probably had since the day they'd met. More and more each day, it had grown. In the last day she'd taken that final plunge and fallen the rest of the way for him.

She held his gaze. "I love you, too."

EPILOGUE

Six months later

Sun shone through the curtains. Beyond the glass, Amy could see the rocker Noah had insisted she have on her front porch. At the horizon, past the city of Denver, was a backdrop of mountains she liked to look at. To bask in the sunshine.

It had been months since she'd been cold, and she was content to let things stay that way for a good long while. Even hiking was different now, though she still enjoyed it.

Because Noah came with her.

She turned and surveyed the furniture. A group of couples from church had come over and helped her get all moved in to her new house. The one Noah would move into with her in a month, after their wedding.

The last few months getting to know each other better than they ever had before, now that she was no longer part of the Witness Security program, had been the best of her life.

All those cartel guys who weren't dead had been arrested. The money they'd been chasing was nothing but a line item on the FBI's accounting of the case—cash Jeremiah had blown and then blamed on her.

The only dark cloud in that sunny sky was the fact

her nephew still hadn't replied to any of her letters. She'd been hoping he would contact her so she could try and repair their relationship. The threat was over now, but he still hadn't responded.

Maybe that wasn't to be.

Amy lifted her chin. She should put a pot of coffee on while she waited for Noah to show up, so they could have dinner. He'd gone to return the rental truck. He was picking up dinner on the way. He'd insisted she didn't need to drive him to his car, and it hadn't made sense, but she hadn't wanted to start an argument with him. Not on a day when they were starting the next phase of their life together. In a place they would call *theirs*.

A knock on the door sounded as she was pouring the water into the coffee maker. Amy set the carafe down carefully and moved to open the front door.

She smiled as she opened it, feeling the joy of how far her life had come. "You're back."

He didn't come inside. She could see her happiness reflected in his eyes, but he wasn't exactly smiling.

"What is—"

Noah took a step closer to her and pressed a kiss to her lips. "I'll give you two a minute." Then he moved past her and she saw who was standing on her doorstep. *Their* doorstep.

"Anthony."

He was tall. Taller than her, and taller than his father. That lanky body of a teenage boy with two hollow legs and a basketball scholarship.

Tears filled her eyes.

He cracked a smile, and then called out, "I told you she was gonna cry."

Amy stepped back. "You two planned this."

"Yep." He came in, and his expression sobered. "I should start by saying sorry. I said awful things to you because I was angry." He took a breath. "The marshals had me see a shrink. He helped me figure out that I lashed out, and it wasn't because I blamed you. You were just an easy target."

"It's okay."

"No, it isn't." He shook his head. "I'm sorry. Noah told me about my dad, and what he did to you."

She pressed her lips together as the tears fell. She hadn't cried for her brother in weeks, but the grief was there at the surface. For what he'd given up. For the pain he'd caused so many. An entire town had been held hostage, all because he'd been content to string along a cartel just for the chance to kill her.

"Auntie Amy... I missed you."

She choked back a sob. He opened his arms and she rushed forward to hug him. So strong. Her nephew was here.

She could hardly believe it.

"I want to live in your guest bedroom until school starts. If you'll let me." His chest shook, like he was laughing. Probably because it was better than crying.

She leaned back. "You do?"

"Not just because I'm a broke college student. But... I'd like to spend time with you." He glanced at Noah, then back at her. "Until you guys are married, anyway."

She looked at Noah. Was he worried about her being here by herself? Maybe, and this was probably the best answer she could ever have thought of. "I love you."

Noah smiled. "You're welcome."

"Don't get all mushy." Anthony groaned. "There will be ground rules."

Amy laughed. She'd thought she was full of joy before. Now it overflowed.

* * * * *

Dear Reader,

This story was a fast and fun romp through snowy Colorado. I hope you enjoyed reading it as much as I enjoyed crafting these characters and watching them navigate the disparity between our dreams and how life goes.

Thankfully, we serve a God who knows our deepest desires and joys in blessing us.

How wonderful is He?

You can find out more about me by visiting my website at www.authorlisaphillips.com.

In Him,

Lisa Phillips

TWIN PURSUIT

Jenna Night

To my mom, Esther. You were always up for an adventure!

The fear of man bringeth a snare:
but whoso putteth his trust in the Lord shall be safe.
—Proverbs 29:25

ONE

Bounty hunter Lauren Dillard strode into the diner in Sweetwater, Colorado, packing a pistol, a can of pepper spray and a set of handcuffs.

The Wagon Wheel Diner was a cozy little restaurant with red upholstered booths and the mellow sounds of classic country music twanging softly in the background. All Lauren had to do to wrap up her assignment was get a close-up look at her quarry to confirm she had the right guy. Then she'd wait until he finished eating, follow him out into the parking lot and slap the cuffs on him.

She took a quick glance out the plate glass window, looking beyond the road and the old redbrick buildings alongside it. Dark clouds loomed in the distance. Soon this bedraggled little town would get a fresh dumping of snow. But she would be on her way back to Denver, just over an hour's drive away, with her bounty by then.

She shifted her gaze back to the inside of the diner, scanning until she spotted her prey. There he was, seated on a swivel stool at the counter, the guy she'd been tailing since early this morning. His name was Matthew Cortez.

The company that hired Lauren had put up a ten-thousand-dollar bond for Mr. Cortez. He was supposed to have appeared in court yesterday to face charges of being an accessory to murder. Matthew had not shown up. The owners of Gold Standard Bail Bonds needed him apprehended, otherwise they'd have to forfeit the bond money to the court.

Lauren wore a heavy cardigan-style sweater over her jeans and long-sleeved T-shirt. The equipment she needed to make her capture was attached to a belt under the loose, unbuttoned sweater where it was out of sight. Some bounty hunters liked to dress dramatically, and it worked for them. Lauren went for an understated look that helped shore up the element of surprise when she went in for the catch.

"Sit anywhere, honey," a waitress called out as she hurried by with four plates of burgers and fries balanced on her arms.

"Thanks." Lauren's heart began racing as she moved toward the counter. It was almost time for the part of her job that she loved the most. That moment of truth, when the person who thought they could flee their responsibilities found out that they could *not*. Her mouth felt dry and her hand trembled with the adrenaline surge as she reached for her phone. She took one last look at the screen where she'd saved a photo of Matthew, just to be sure it was him, even though she'd already memorized that image of black hair, tanned skin and dark brown eyes.

Lauren had studied that picture countless times since yesterday morning, when she'd gotten the call to track him. She and her business partner, Kevin, had checked the home address located in Denver that Matthew had listed on his bond application. It was the same address shown on the photocopy of his driver's license in his file, but it had turned out to be a Laundromat tucked in a residential part of town. A little further investigation had proven that the driver's license was fake.

Research conducted into the very early hours of this morning had turned up an old address for Matthew at a small ranch here in Sweetwater. She and Kevin were scheduled to meet up and make the drive over before sunrise this morning. But then Kevin's dad had been rushed to the hospital for chest pains. Of course the right thing was for Kevin to go and be with his dad. So Lauren had made the drive here alone. She could grab Matthew by herself, and if he gave her trouble during the transport back to Denver, she'd call for backup and wait for one of the other bounty hunters employed by Gold Standard to come and help her out.

She'd waited outside the ranch, studying Matthew's picture, wary of approaching the residence, since she'd had no idea how many people were staying at the property. And she knew he was associated with a very dangerous group of people. Eventually a blue pickup truck had exited the property. The driver had looked like Matthew, but he wore a black cowboy hat pulled down low in front, and it was hard to say for certain if it was him. If she jumped the gun and tried to grab the wrong person, he would obviously alert Matthew as soon as he was released. Matthew would take off for parts unknown and she'd be back to square one.

She'd held back and followed him into the town of Sweetwater, where he'd made several stops. They'd all been places where she couldn't follow him in for a better look without being noticed.

When people initially violated their bond, it wasn't unusual for them to visit their regular haunts. Some of them didn't seem to realize that skipping their court date was a big deal. And after they were apprehended, they would claim that they'd gotten their court date confused and hadn't realized they'd violated their bond.

Whatever. Lauren just knew she'd found Matthew fairly easily, and she didn't want to blow her chance at grabbing him. So she'd waited until he'd pulled into the parking lot at the diner to make her move.

Now she had him. He'd taken off the hat. She just needed to get a good look at his face to be sure.

She sat down on a padded stool at the counter, ordered a cup of black coffee and a slice of pecan pie with ice cream, and took a couple of deep breaths to slow her racing heart. From the corner of her eye she saw a waitress set a plate with a patty melt and onion rings in front of him. The same waitress brought her coffee. She took a couple of sips, and her slight headache eased. Then her pie and ice cream arrived. She didn't realize how ravenous she was until she started eating.

All the while, she stole quick glances down the counter toward her target. Finally, he looked in her direction. It was him. Matthew Cortez. She was certain of it. His hair was shorter than it was in the picture and he was clean-shaven now, but it was him. She quickly turned her gaze back to the empty dish in front of her and bit back a triumphant smile. *Enjoy your last few minutes of freedom, pal. You're headed back to jail.*

"Mama, I want spaghetti for my birthday lunch!" an excited little girl shouted right behind Lauren. A second little girl and a boy jostled around beside the birthday girl as the family got situated in a booth. The young mom and dad looked frazzled but happy. They also had an infant in a carrier.

This sweet family was within twenty feet of a wanted criminal, and they had no clue. Along with the current accessory-to-murder charges, Matthew had some old assault charges and an illegal weapons–possession charge that he'd served time for. He also had some recent large-scale theft charges that he'd somehow managed to beat at trial. He was a violent thug. He needed to be locked up. People needed to be kept safe. Lauren could help with that. It was why she loved her job.

She texted Al, the bail bondsman, with an update on the situation. In his response, he let her know that Kevin's dad was going to be okay. She sipped her way through two refills on her coffee, all while keeping a close eye on Matthew.

Finally, he finished eating and set a few dollars beside his plate as he stood up to leave. It felt like he slowed down as he passed behind her on his way to the cashier, but maybe that was just her imagination.

Her heart started racing again. And it wasn't just from the caffeine. It was that thrill of the hunt that made her look forward to going to work every day.

She wouldn't turn around and look at him. Not just yet. She could see a vague reflection of him in the glass in a nearby picture frame, so she knew where he was.

Finally, she glanced over her shoulder and saw him getting his change back from the cashier. It was go time. She stood up, grabbed a twenty from her pocket and tossed it on the counter. She didn't have time to deal with the cashier. She needed to catch up with her target.

The glass door at the front of the diner was falling shut behind him just as Lauren got to it. She hesitated, glancing through the glass to see if he was waiting there to jump her. He wasn't.

He was walking to his truck in the parking lot. Perfect. She walked outside, picking up her pace, adrenaline sparking energy throughout her body, ready to do whatever was necessary to get this violent criminal off the streets.

"Mathew Cortez," she yelled out as she got closer to him. "Stop right there!"

* * *

Matthew. It had been a long time since anyone had called Jason Cortez by that name.

A flicker of nostalgia came and went. Times changed. People changed. There was never any going back.

He turned around and saw a woman heading purposefully toward him. Of course he recognized her from the counter in the diner. She'd been sitting only a few stools away from him. Even if she'd been farther away, he would have noticed her.

Four years had passed since he'd returned stateside after serving in the army in Afghanistan, but the habit of situational awareness, of paying attention to his surroundings, had not completely gone away. And it had its benefits. Fortunately, the hyperalertness that triggered panic attacks had finally faded after he'd been stateside for two years.

Thank You, Lord. He offered up a short, silent prayer, just as he did nearly every time he thought of those harrowing couple of years. Without his faith, he might not have made it through that time.

"You've mistaken me for someone else," he said to the woman as she drew closer to him.

She was cute, with amber-colored eyes, dark blond hair pulled back in a ponytail and a light scattering of freckles across the bridge of her nose and her cheeks. Her skin was already turning red from the cold air. She looked like an earnest type of woman who was probably in student government when she was in high school. She certainly didn't look like the type of woman who would want anything to do with Matt Cortez.

She was also carrying a pistol, he guessed, after noticing the bulging drape of her sweater at her waistband and the way her hand kept hovering near it. If that were the case—if she went through life armed with a deadly weapon—then she just might be the kind of woman who'd be looking for Matt, after all.

"Nice try, but I haven't made a mistake," she said. "I know exactly who you are, Matthew, and you're under arrest for failing to appear before the court in Denver yesterday morning to face charges of accessory to murder. Your bond is forfeited."

"Who exactly are you?" he asked, realization slowly dawning on him. "Some kind of bounty hunter?"

"My name is Lauren Dillard. And yes, I'm a bounty hunter." She reached beneath her sweater and removed a pair of handcuffs that had been attached to her belt.

"Well, you're making a mistake, Lauren." He crossed his arms over his chest. "My name is Jason Cortez. Matthew is my brother. We're identical twins."

He maintained a neutral expression even as his heart dropped to his feet. *Accessory to murder.* Matt seemed determined to throw his life away. There was no denying that he'd become a dangerous man. He'd been arrested several times. More recently for charges ranging from commercial burglary to highway cargo theft to assault.

And somebody, somewhere, had put forth the money to hire a very good lawyer to keep Matt from doing serious time in prison on those recent charges. That fact worried Jason the most. Because he knew the unknown person would want something from Matt in return.

"I'm not buying your story about being an identical twin, though you do get points for creativity," the bounty hunter said. "Now turn around and put your hands behind your back."

"No. Why don't *you* turn around, head back to the bail bonds office you work for and do some research." He wasn't angry, but he was getting annoyed. "You'll find out Matt has a twin brother. Better yet, take a picture of me. Then compare it to whatever picture you have of Matt. He has a scar over his left eye. I don't."

She bit her lower lip for a second, like she was considering what he'd said. Then she arched an eyebrow. "I'm going to cuff you and take you down to the local police department. They can run your fingerprints. And if you are not Matthew Cortez, they'll know."

Not a chance. Jason had places to be this afternoon. His welding business was just starting to pick up momentum, and he still had a couple more appointments scheduled to do some on-site metal repairs before the day was over. Why should he waste his time just because this *bounty hunter* targeted the wrong Cortez brother?

"Like I said, do your research." He reached into his pocket for his keys.

The bounty hunter went for the canister of pepper spray attached to her belt.

He could appreciate that she was just trying to do her job. But he was not going with her. He was not going to let her pepper spray him. And he did not want to hurt her.

He let go of his keys and eased his hand out of his pocket. He needed to get control of this situation, and he had to move quickly. He'd grab her arms before she could target him with the pepper spray.

The sound of a car engine roaring up the driveway into the diner parking lot followed by the squealing of brakes caught his attention. He turned in time to see a black sedan with its windows rolled down. And then he saw a glint of metal pointing out of the space where the passenger window would have been.

"Gun!"

The shots exploded at the same time that Jason and

the bounty hunter both hit the deck, pressing themselves down onto the icy asphalt.

Screams and shouts sounded across the parking lot, along with the scuffling of other people taking cover.

Jason's heart pounded in his chest. At the same time, his military training kicked in. He forced his thoughts to stay logical and focused. Shielded by his pickup truck, he got to his feet, but he stayed in a squatting positing so he'd keep out of sight of the shooter.

The bounty hunter likewise got to her feet but stayed squatting down. She had her pistol in her hand instead of the pepper spray. "Who are your friends?" she asked, glaring at him.

He shook his head. "I have no idea who they are." But if he had to guess, they were people who, like the bounty hunter, had mistaken him for his twin brother. In fact, this bounty hunter might have led them directly to him.

"Cortez! You still alive?" a voice called out from the direction of the sedan. Jason could hear the car's engine idling. "This is what we do to traitors," the voice shouted again. "We finish them off." Then he heard the sound of a car door opening and slamming shut, followed by the sound of footsteps crunching across the blacktop. The shooter was coming after him.

The bounty hunter started to raise her gun. She looked toward the back of Jason's truck, the direction where it sounded like the footsteps were coming from. She started to move, and it looked to Jason like she was going to confront the shooter.

"Lauren, wait!" he called out in a loud whisper. Another time and another place, he'd be all about a full-out attack on anyone who'd attacked him first. But there were kids in that diner. For all he knew, there were kids crouched down with their parents right now in this freezing-cold parking lot. He didn't have a gun with him. But even if he did, he wouldn't want a gunfight in a parking lot. Not if there was any possible way to avoid it. Once a bullet was fired, you couldn't control where it went. He didn't want to risk anyone getting hit.

The bounty hunter turned to him, her brows furrowed and her eyes tense with impatience.

He shook his head. "There's no need for a shoot-out here." Still crouched down, he reached up and quietly opened the passenger door of his truck. He took off his cowboy hat and tossed it in. "I'm going to drive out of here. They obviously think I'm my brother. They'll follow me. I'm sure somebody's called the cops by now. You stay here, make sure the gunman doesn't go into the diner. When the cops get here, tell them what you saw."

Hopefully, the gunmen hadn't gotten a good look at the bounty hunter and didn't think she was somehow connected to Matt. But maybe they had seen her, and maybe they'd target her as a way to get to Matt. "Be careful," Jason warned.

"What exactly is it you think you're going to do?" she asked.

He nodded his head toward the exit on the other side of the parking lot. "I'm going to drive out that way. Lead them out of town and away from people." And he'd pray the police would find him and the shooters who were chasing him before things got too far out of hand.

She nodded and then used her free hand to once again reach for the pepper spray. Good. Maybe that meant she'd leave off using the gun unless she absolutely had to.

"You and I still have unfinished business," she said to him. "Matthew or *Jason* or whoever you are. I'll find you again. And we'll straighten things out. Now go!"

Jason climbed into the passenger seat of his truck. He

glanced out the window just as the gunman spotted him and started running toward him. Which meant he would also be running toward Lauren.

Despite Jason's intention to lead the fight away from the parking lot, he couldn't leave the bounty hunter to face the gunman on her own. He got out of the truck in time to see her spring up from the spot where she'd been hidden and fire pepper spray into the shooter's face, temporarily blinding him.

The guy started screaming and swearing, stumbling around and covering his eyes with his free arm while wildly firing his gun. Several of the rounds went into Jason's truck, near the engine, before the guy finally smacked his hand on a side-view mirror. His weapon flew out of his hand and slid under the truck.

Meanwhile the black sedan was creeping closer, the driver screaming to the shooter, who had now dropped to his knees and was trying to retrieve his gun.

Jason looked around for the bounty hunter. He spotted her racing across the parking lot, away from the black sedan. Good. She was getting out of the way where she'd be safe.

The driver got out of the sedan, carrying a pistol and screaming threats as he headed toward Jason. "You're dead, Matt Cortez. Dead!"

Jason reached into the bed of his truck, where he kept his work tools. He put his hand on a heavy wrench and pulled it out. If the shooters caught up with him, he'd use it as a club. Not the best weapon to have when facing an enraged guy with a gun, but it was something.

Meanwhile, he could still follow through with his plans to draw the bad guys away from the diner. He'd just have to do it on foot. He started moving away from his truck, staying crouched down and shielded by the parked cars and trucks. He scurried away from the shooters and toward the exit on the other side of the lot. Eventually he would run out of cover. He could only hope that neither of the thugs was a particularly good shot.

He reached the edge of the parking lot just as a dark green SUV pulled up in front of him on the street and squealed to a halt. The passenger-side window was rolled down. From the driver's seat, the bounty hunter gestured furiously at him, yelling, *"Get in!"*

Jason hesitated for a split second. Behind him he could hear the gunmen hollering. They were bound to start shooting again at any second. He didn't really know this woman at all. But what other choice did he have? He yanked open the door and climbed in. The bounty hunter hit the gas, and they sped down the road.

TWO

Lauren made quick, random turns down the residential streets of Sweetwater. Not that there were very many streets. Behind her, she could hear the sirens from cop cars arriving back at the diner. She glanced in the rearview mirror. There was no sign of the bad guys in the black sedan behind them. She eased off the gas, and after a couple more turns, she was fairly certain no one was following them. She would call the police later and return to Sweetwater to give them a statement describing what had happened if they needed one from her.

She continued down the road until it led to a wooded area where they were no longer in front of any houses. She steered toward the side of the road, stopped and put the SUV into Park. Then she pulled out her pistol and pointed it at Jason.

He'd been looking at the side mirror. He turned and saw the gun, and his eyes widened. "Easy," he said. "What's going on?"

"Put your hands on the dash. Keep them where I can see them or I'll shoot you." And she was prepared to do that. For all she knew, this guy really was Matthew Cortez and she'd just helped a man who'd participated in a murder get away from the cops. Her own father was a con man—she knew anyone could be fooled by a skilled liar.

"Are you part of some kind of rival criminal gang who's also after my brother?" Jason asked, his voice hardening. "Is that what's going on here?"

"Hands on the dash," she repeated. "Move slowly."

He complied. Glaring at her all the while.

Without taking her eyes off him, she reached into the file folder tucked beside her seat and pulled out a full-size printed picture of Matthew Cortez that had been taken in the bail bond office a couple of weeks ago. She brought it up to eye level so she could glance back and forth between the photo and the man claiming to be Matthew's twin brother.

"If you still thought I might be Matt, why'd you drive me away from the shooters?"

"I'm a bounty hunter, not a vigilante," she said. "I don't want to see anybody shot up by a couple of thugs."

Plus, his concern for the safety of the people in the diner and the parking lot had her thinking he wasn't the hardened criminal she was looking for. But that appearance of concern could have been a calculated ploy to win over her trust.

Now that she was looking at the photo alongside the actual man in the vehicle with her, Lauren could see the difference between the two brothers. Both were handsome men. But along with the scar over his eye, Matthew looked like he'd had his nose broken at some point in his life. He also looked haggard, with a hint of exhaustion in his eyes that said he'd need a lot more than just a few nights' sleep to have the same robust look of good health that his twin brother had.

"Okay, I believe you. You aren't Matthew Cortez."

Lauren tucked the picture back into the folder and holstered her gun.

Blowing out an audible sigh of relief, Jason leaned back in his seat. All the while, he kept his gaze locked on her.

"Tell me where I can find your brother," she said.

"I don't know where he is. It's been a long time since I talked to him. I think he still lives in Denver, but I don't know that for certain."

"He gave us a fake home address on his bond application. What's his real address?"

Jason shook his head. "I don't remember his actual address, but I might remember how to get to his apartment if I went to Denver."

Lauren sighed. "Let's exchange phone numbers. I'm sure I'll have questions for you as I get further into the hunt. And if you think of something that might help, call me."

He gave her his number and she tapped it into her phone.

"You can go now," she finally said, waving her hand toward the car door beside him.

He raised his dark eyebrows. "That's it? That's all you have to say?"

She shrugged. "What more do you want? I rescued you from a couple of killers. You're welcome. Now, get out of my car. I still need to find my bounty."

"Rescued me?" he said, crossing his arms over his chest but otherwise not moving. "You led those people directly to me. *You* put me in danger."

"No." She shook her head. "I tracked you for hours this morning. Nobody was tailing me. They found you on their own. I should probably say they found the man who they believe is Matthew Cortez on their own. I un-

derstand you not wanting to walk the streets of Sweet-
water with a couple of gunmen on the lookout for you, so
I'll drop you off somewhere. Maybe the police station?
I wouldn't go back to that ranch right away. If I know
Matthew used to stay there, the thugs who are after him
probably know that, too."

He stared at her with an expression she'd seen countless times before, and it triggered a warm feeling in the
center of her chest. It was the look of a man who'd just
realized he'd underestimated her. She never got tired of
seeing it.

"You're going to continue tracking Matt?" he asked.

"Of course." She was shaken up by the shooting in
the parking lot. She wasn't going to lie to herself about
that. *Thank You, Lord, for protecting me.* She glanced at
Jason and amended her prayer. *Thank You for protecting us.* But even though she was still unsettled, still felt
her heart beating faster than usual thanks to the adrenaline rush, she wasn't going to give up. "I get paid when I
bring in my bounty," she said. "And like everybody else,
I need to make a living."

He sat there with his hands resting on his thighs, the
fingers of his right hand tapping his leg. He stared out
the front windshield for what was only a minute, but it
felt longer. Light snowflakes started to fall, melting as
soon as they hit the glass. "I don't want you to drop me
off somewhere," he finally said. His tone was filled with
dread. "I want to go with you. I'll help you find him."

"Yeah, right." Lauren shook her head. "Like I'm going
to have you tagging along, giving your brother a heads-
up whenever I get close to him so he can get away. Not
going to happen."

"I won't do that."

"He's your brother. Your *identical twin* brother. Of course you will. People protect members of their family."

At least that was how it usually worked in Lauren's experience. Although her own father had apparently never gotten the memo on that. He hadn't made any effort to look out for Lauren or her mom. She shook off that train of thought. Dwelling on it didn't change anything.

"The best way I can protect my brother is by helping you find him," Jason said. He shifted position slightly so he was turned toward her. "I know he's connected with a criminal group. And the shooter yelled something about Matt being a traitor. I don't know what's going on, but it's obviously bad. And dangerous."

"So you want to help him escape and hide until things die down."

"No." Jason took in a deep breath and blew it out. "Look, if he actually had something to do with a murder, then he needs to face charges for that. Even if he's innocent, he still needs to face the charges. Obey the law. Do the right thing."

He shook his head. "Matt *has* to change the way he's been living. This might be my last chance to help him. And I want to make sure he shows up in court. Owns up to whatever he's done. Maybe helping you catch him and getting him back in jail will prevent a cop from getting hurt." He sighed. "I don't know how Matt will behave if he's backed into a corner by a police officer. I barely know him anymore."

Lauren looked into his eyes. She had to make a decision, and she decided she believed him. Would he change his tune when they finally caught up with his brother? Give him some kind of warning? Misdirect her during a chase? Maybe. But it was also possible that he'd rather see his brother locked up than dead.

"All right," she said. "But you'll have to earn your keep."

He tilted his head slightly. "And how would you like me to do that?"

"Give me some leads on how to find your brother. Tell me some things I don't already know."

"I can do that. And I can watch your back."

That brought to mind something she'd noticed earlier when the bullets had started flying in the diner parking lot. "You kept your head back there," she said. "It looked like you'd been shot at before."

"Six years in the United States Army," he said.

That experience would be helpful. All the more reason to let him tag along with her while she hunted his brother.

"Good. That means you know how to take orders," she said, pulling back out onto the road and picking up speed.

He let out a short laugh. "Yeah, well, I've gotten a little rusty when it comes to that."

Riding down the highway, Jason wished that he was the one driving. Not that Lauren was doing a bad job, it was just that he was used to being in control.

They were halfway to Denver and reaching the edge of the storm clouds that were still sending down snow. But the snowfall was light here and it wasn't collecting on the highway, so they were making good time.

"Still nothing from your brother?" Lauren asked.

Jason glanced at his phone screen. "Still no answer."

As soon as they were clear of Sweetwater, he'd called Matt and left a voice mail message telling him that he needed a return call and that it was important. Then he'd sent a text.

Maybe Matt hadn't gotten the messages yet. Maybe he was too drunk or high to respond. Maybe he just didn't care anymore.

Jason shifted his gaze to the side-view mirror and watched to see if they were being followed. It didn't seem likely, but what did he know? He still couldn't believe that Lauren had been tailing *him* from the time he'd left the ranch this morning. He'd already seen that she was good at her job, but still, the fact that she'd watched him without his knowing nipped at his pride.

"Tell me about the places where your brother spends time," Lauren said. "Maybe he's mentioned the names of friends he's hung out with, girlfriends he visits, nightclubs he frequents. Anything could help. We can't waste time. If he hasn't called you back by the time we hit Denver, we need to start looking somewhere. Whoever sent those shooters is probably still looking for him to kill him."

The sad thing was, he didn't know much about his brother's life. He knew of a couple of his past girlfriends but didn't know if he had one now. The brother he used to know liked Mexican food, dirt bikes and spy novels. None of that helped, and it might not even be true anymore.

His phone rang. He looked at the screen. It was Matt. His pulse jumped.

"People are trying to kill you," Jason said into the phone, forgoing any conventional greeting and hoping that his warning would grab Matt's attention.

There was a pause, and then Matt laughed. "What else is new?" he said sourly.

"There were two shooters in Sweetwater. They fired at me thinking I was you."

Matt swore. "Were you hit?"

"No."

"Good. Keep your head down."

"Wait!" Jason said, because it sounded like Matt was

about to disconnect. "I'm on my way to Denver. I want to meet up with you."

"Why?"

Lauren glanced over at him as she drove, clearly listening closely to the conversation and trying to figure out what was going on.

"I've got to go somewhere. I can't go back to the ranch. Someone might be waiting for me there. They aren't going to give me time to explain that I'm not you before they start shooting. Maybe you can tell me what's going on. Maybe we can come up with a plan."

"You coming alone?" Matt asked, a hint of suspicion in his tone.

Jason glanced over at Lauren. Did he lie to his brother or did he admit he was bringing someone along? Obviously if he said he had a bounty hunter with him, his brother would be long gone by the time they got there. And if he were honest with himself, maybe some part of him wanted that. Maybe he wanted Matt to get away. Maybe he wasn't strong enough to help send his brother to prison.

He and Matt had been eight years old when Matt got that distinctive scar over his eye. They were playing in the mud at the ranch with little metal cars and trucks, maneuvering the chipped and dented toy vehicles as they climbed over boulders and fallen trees. Jason had gotten mad about some dumb thing. He'd flung his car at his brother, and they'd both been astonished when it hit him and split the skin above his eye, blood running out of the wound. Of course their dad was nowhere to be found.

Matt never got the stitches he'd needed. And he never seemed to hold a grudge about the scar that had been the result.

Matt had done a lot of bad things, but he had never

intentionally betrayed Jason. And what Jason was doing right now—betraying Matt's trust—could put an end to their tattered relationship.

But not following through with his plan could lead to Matt ending up dead at the hands of his fellow criminals.

"You still there?" Matt asked.

"Yeah, I'm here. You still at the same apartment?" Jason asked, feeling queasy even though he believed he was doing the right thing.

He heard noise on Matt's end of the call. It sounded like other people were there, and Jason felt his body tense. Other people there could make things go haywire when he and Lauren showed up.

"I'm still living at the same place," Matt finally said. There was more noise. People were there in his apartment. Or maybe it was just the TV. It was hard to tell. "I'll see ya," Matt said, and then he disconnected.

Jason relayed the full conversation to Lauren.

"If you want, I can drop you off somewhere after you show me Matt's apartment," Lauren offered as they reached the outskirts of Denver. "You don't have to be there when I apprehend him."

Jason shook his head. "He's a smart man. He'll figure out what happened."

"He might guess, but he won't *know* you helped me find him. I won't tell him."

"Yeah, well, I have to be there. It might be my last chance to talk to my brother. Ever." There was no going back now. He had to grab whatever opportunity presented itself to convince Matt that he was doing this because he cared about him.

"I understand," Lauren said. "And I know this is hard."

"He might not be alone," Jason said, realizing he should have mentioned that sooner.

"What? Who's there with him? How many people?" Lauren's tone changed. She was back to the way she was when she'd first spoken to him, impersonal and professional.

"I heard voices," he said. "Two or three. But it might have just been a TV."

Lauren nodded. "To be safe, I'll call for backup as soon as we get to Matt's apartment."

This could turn out to be a long night. Jason called his neighbor in Sweetwater and asked if he'd go over to the ranch and make sure his dogs, barn cats and horses were okay and that they had food and water. He didn't have much in the way of livestock to worry about. The place was a ranch in name only these days.

The neighbor was happy to help.

Dusky shadows were forming between buildings as they rolled into the city. Lauren made a call alerting someone to be on standby to help apprehend a bail jumper. She told them she'd call with a specific address when she had one and then disconnected.

Jason told her when they were nearing the freeway exit where they needed to turn off.

"When's the last time you visited your brother?" she asked as they waited at a traffic light.

Jason looked around to get his bearings, searching for landmarks. When they started moving again, he saw a grocery store and a doughnut shop he recognized. They were on the right track. "It was about a year and a half ago." He'd still been dealing with a lot of anxiety back then. Matt, on the other hand, had seemed very detached. Probably an effect of the drugs he was using.

He directed her to take a couple more turns. "Slow down," he finally said. "It's up here on the left."

She pulled over just short of reaching the apartment

complex and parked at the curb on the opposite side of the street. She called her people and gave them the address and told them she'd wait for their arrival.

"They should be here in about fifteen minutes," she said after disconnecting.

Meanwhile, Jason stared at the apartments. Why hadn't he come here to visit Matt more often? Why hadn't he pushed a relationship on his brother, even if Matt didn't want one?

"Which apartment is your brother's?" Lauren asked.

"Downstairs, on the right."

"Do you see his vehicle?"

"No. Parking is in the back."

"When everybody gets here, we'll break into teams," Lauren said. "Someone will go with me to the front door. Two people will go behind the building in case he tries to run out the back. Once we've got him secured, you can talk to him. Then we'll turn him in to the police, and it will be over."

Jason got out of the SUV.

"What are you doing?" Lauren called out sharply.

The smart thing would be to hold back and wait. Jason didn't have a weapon. Didn't know his brother's state of mind. Wasn't sure who was in the apartment with Matt.

And yet, he found himself walking toward his brother's front door.

THREE

I shouldn't have trusted him.

Lauren took several jogging steps to catch up with Jason. He was tall, his strides were long and he was moving quickly.

Like an idiot, she'd let her guard down with him because he had nice manners. And he'd looked her in the eye when they'd talked about apprehending his brother, giving her the impression that he was honest. And admittedly, there was something about him that caught her attention on a personal level. A hint of attraction that had clouded her judgment.

She knew better than to let that happen. And from now on, she'd make it a point to keep her emotional distance from him.

"Hey!" she called out, but not too loudly. She didn't want to risk Matt hearing a commotion outside, looking out the window and realizing something was up. He'd take off, and she could lose him.

"I'm going to go knock on the door," Jason said reasonably, focused on his brother's apartment and not even turning to look at her. "I'll act like I came here alone and I just want to talk to him. You wait for your backup. If there's anybody else in the apartment with him, I'll look out the window. That'll be your signal so you're prepared for that. I want to do this as calmly as possible."

It wasn't a bad idea. But it wasn't *her* idea, and having Jason take control of the situation was not in her plans. This was *her* capture. She'd brought him along because he might be of help to her. She didn't want him getting too comfortable giving orders.

Her phone vibrated. At the same time, she heard and then saw an SUV pull up on the side of the street behind her own vehicle. She looked at the screen and saw a text from Toby letting her know that he and Tim had arrived. That was fast.

"Hold up," she called out to Jason. They were just about to pass by the corner of the apartment building. Once they were beyond it, anyone looking out the front window of Matt's unit would see them. "My people are here," she said. "Let me get them in place in the back of the building before you knock on Matt's door."

"You do what you feel you have to," Jason said without breaking stride.

She stopped and let him continue on without her. She got Toby on the phone and brought him up to speed. Then she directed him to take Tim with him and cut through a grassy passage between the apartment building and a duplex next door to it so they could get in position behind the apartments.

Before they could get into position, she heard Jason knock on Matt's door. She moved away from the hedge to get a clearer view. There were a few lights outside the building, but there were still plenty of shadows, so she was partially hidden. A familiar emotion—a combination of nerves and high-voltage excitement—swirled around in the pit of her stomach. This moment, before a capture, gave her the sense of focus and purpose that she loved.

Jason knocked again. "Matt, open up. It's me."

Light from an outside fixture reflected on the front window, making it hard to tell if there were any lights burning inside the apartment.

Jason knocked again. He waited, then turned his head and pressed his ear against the door to listen. A few seconds passed, and he pulled his head away from the door. He knocked again and then started pounding on the door. "Matt! Open the door!"

Lauren's muscles tensed, and a sense of unease crept up her spine. Something was wrong. Matt might have been suspicious after Jason's call. Maybe he was hiding from them.

A door to one of the other apartments was yanked open, and someone shouted words Lauren couldn't quite understand.

Jason took off jogging around the corner toward the back of the building, disappearing out of sight.

What was he doing? Lauren sprinted after him. From the back of the building she heard a jumble of voices shouting, and then she clearly heard Toby yelling, "Get on the ground! Now!"

They must have found Matt climbing out a back window and the hunt was over. Good. It had been a long day, and she was exhausted. She rounded the corner of the building.

It turned out that the hunt wasn't over.

Jason hadn't obeyed Toby's command to get on the ground. But in the illumination from Tim's flashlight, she could see that Jason did have his hands up. And he kept glancing warily at the canister of pepper spray in Toby's hand.

"Is everybody all right?" Lauren asked.

Jason turned to Lauren, his anger evident in the hard

line of his mouth before he spoke. "You couldn't tell your backup that Matt had an identical twin walking around out here?" he snapped.

"You couldn't follow directions?" she snapped back. "If you had, they would have met you before we all moved to surround the apartment building and this would not have happened." She turned to her fellow bounty hunters. "Guys, this is Jason Cortez. This isn't Matthew."

Toby put away his pepper spray, and Jason lowered his hands.

"Sorry, man," Tim said, turning his flashlight away from Jason's face.

"And yes, I did let them know about you," Lauren said. "In a text I sent to the bail bond office earlier today when I let them know what was going on."

"We couldn't be sure which twin you were," Tim added. "You really are identical."

"What's going on back here?" a voice called out, followed by the wash of light from a flashlight. "Do I need to call the cops?"

The person talking drew closer. Lauren realized it was the guy who'd yelled earlier when Jason was pounding on Matt's door. He was a short, heavyset man wearing a thick coat.

He shone his light on each person's face until he got to Jason. "Hey, where have you been?" he demanded. "I'm tired of all these people looking for you. You owe 'em money or something?"

"I'm not Matt," Jason said. "I'm his twin brother."

The guy stared at him for a minute. Finally Lauren jumped in, assuring the guy that Jason was not Matt.

"Well, I'm your brother's landlord," the guy said. "I've been waiting for him to show up for two weeks now. As soon as he does, I'm giving him notice to move out. Too many creeps hang out around the building when he's here, and now he's got some scary-looking people coming by asking about him. That's why I yelled at you to go away when I first heard you knocking on his door. I thought you were one of them."

"What can you tell me about those people?" Lauren asked.

The landlord shrugged and crossed his arms over his chest. Now that the sun was gone, the temperature was dropping fast. "Just that they showed up a few times looking for him. They asked the other tenants if they'd seen him. They were polite enough, but kind of intense."

"Could we have a look in his apartment?" Jason asked. "That might give us an idea of where he is. Or if anything happened to him. We talked earlier today and agreed to meet here tonight."

When he agreed to meet with you, he was lying to you, Lauren thought. Jason didn't want to face the obvious truth that his brother had lied to him. She knew how that felt. Her dad had lied to her all the time. But she resisted the temptation to feel bad for him. He wasn't her friend. She was standing here beside him because they were working a case together.

"I won't *let* you into his apartment," the manager said. "I could get sued or lose my job. But I might accidentally leave his door unlocked." He shook his finger at Jason. "I will be watching, though. I don't want anybody stealing from any of my tenants. So if I see anybody carrying anything out, I'm calling the cops."

Jason nodded. "Understood."

The manager took some keys out of his pocket and headed back toward the front of the building, presumably to go unlock Matt's door.

"I'm leaving," Tim said as soon as the manager was

out of earshot. He glanced at Toby, who nodded in agreement, then he looked at Lauren. "You know I'm all about getting the job done, but what they're talking about is too close to breaking and entering. I'm not going to risk getting busted for that."

"I was thinking the same thing," she said. The fee she earned for tracking down Matt would help pay the rent this month, but at the end of the day, it was just one case. There would be others.

They all started walking around the building. When they reached the front, Tim and Toby said their goodbyes and walked toward their SUV.

Jason was already headed for his brother's apartment.

"I'm waiting out here," Lauren called to him, standing outside the door. "Let me know what you find in there."

It sounded like he said, "Right," as he disappeared into the apartment, closing the door behind him. But did he mean it sarcastically, as in fat chance he'd tell her? Or did he mean he really would tell her?

She wrestled with the temptation to go in there with him and see for herself. But Jason was Matt's family. She obviously was not. He was checking on his brother's welfare. That was not exactly her motivation. There was a line there that she couldn't cross.

She should have told Jason to leave the apartment door open. Although now that she knew him better, she realized that he might not have done it.

"Dear Lord, please let Matt be okay." Jason whispered the prayer as he walked quickly through the apartment, searching the rooms, dreading the moment when he would find his brother's lifeless body. It was the fear that he'd lived with over the last few years as his brother had fallen deeper into his criminal lifestyle.

But Matt was not in the apartment. The thermostat for the heater had been turned down, and the place was cold. There was no recent mail on the countertop with the unopened bills. The sliced turkey and potato salad in the fridge were definitely beyond their expiration dates. Everything in the smelly kitchen trash can had obviously been there for a while.

It looked like the landlord's story was true and that Matt hadn't been here for days. He'd lied to Jason when they were on the phone and he'd confirmed he was home. But why? He could have just told Jason it wasn't a good time for him to stop by. He hadn't been shy about doing that in the past.

Jason walked through the apartment again, looking for signs of a break-in or a struggle, but he didn't see anything. There were still clothes hanging in the closet and an expensive pair of cowboy boots sitting on the closet floor. Matt hadn't skipped out to avoid paying rent. It wouldn't make sense to do that and leave everything behind. And money was not usually a problem for Matt. He always found a way to get some.

"Hey, what do you see?" Lauren hollered through the front door.

"Nobody's here," he hollered back.

There were a few empty beer bottles on the coffee table and the place reeked of weed. The strong smell saturated the upholstered furniture and the drapes. Otherwise things looked normal. There was no sign that Matt was using harder drugs, so that was encouraging. There was nothing flashy or expensive in sight. Whatever money he got from his criminal enterprises seemed to disappear pretty fast. It was hard to believe Matt would break the law and risk prison time for such an average kind of life.

"Any idea where your brother went?" Lauren called out to him.

"He didn't leave a note," Jason called back.

"Funny." She didn't sound genuinely amused.

Jason walked over to the door and pulled it open. "It looks like he's been gone for at least a few days," he said. "But it also looks like he plans on coming back."

He walked out and pulled the door shut behind him, making sure it was locked. From the other side of the building, the manager opened his door and gave him a quick wave before closing the door again.

"Where do you think we should go look for him?" Lauren asked as they crossed the lawn heading back toward her SUV. "You must know some of his friends."

You'd think he would. They'd had a few friends in common when they were younger, but he had no idea who Matt spent time with these days.

A shotgun blast echoed across the front of the apartment building.

Jason threw himself on top of Lauren as shards of glass from nearby light fixtures rained down on them. A second blast followed. And then a third. His heart pounded while at the same time his senses sharpened and his attention focused on his surroundings, on what might be moving in the shadows and on making sure Lauren didn't get hurt.

The sudden darkness following the destruction of the lights was a blessing. Now whoever was shooting at them couldn't see them as clearly.

The shots had come from the direction of the street. Full night had fallen while they were checking out Matt's apartment, and there were no streetlights on this stretch of road. There were only a couple of other light fixtures attached to the building and still functioning, but the light they cast didn't come anywhere near to illuminating the road. They offered just enough light to disrupt Jason's night vision. Even so, he could tell there was a vehicle idling out there. Its lights were off, but he could hear it.

"Are you all right?" Jason asked, his lips not far from Lauren's ear. "Were you hit?"

"I'm fine." She reached for the gun on her hip and tried to roll to her side. "You can get off me."

He started to move, and two more shotgun blasts boomed in the darkness. More glass rained down on them as an upstairs window shattered.

He shifted his weight so that Lauren could reach her gun. She lifted her head, propped up on her elbows and pointed her weapon toward the direction where the shots had come from.

Sirens blared in the distance.

A car engine growled, followed by the screeching sound of quick acceleration as the vehicle peeled off down the street. Jason couldn't get a clear look at it, but he had the impression that it was not the sedan they'd seen earlier today. This was something bigger, like a large SUV or a van.

They got to their feet, and Lauren holstered her pistol.

"We need to go our separate ways," Jason said. "It's too dangerous for anyone to be around me. Obviously, these thugs haven't figured out that I'm not Matt."

"No," she said. "This just makes me that much more determined to get him off the streets. For his own safety. For yours. For the general public. And we'll be more successful if we work together."

The sirens he'd heard were getting closer.

"We need to get you a gun," she said.

Jason had already thought about that. "No," he said, shaking his head. "I'm not going to put myself in a situation where I could end up shooting and killing my brother."

"I understand how you feel," Lauren said. "But that's not a smart decision."

"Maybe it isn't," he said. But he wasn't going to debate the point with her.

Blue and red flashing lights spilled over them as four cop cars pulled up on the scene. Jason and Lauren raised their hands high, just to be safe, as the officers opened their patrol car doors. There'd be plenty of time to explain the fact that they were the people who'd been shot *at* after the scene was secure and the tension level dropped.

Behind them, Jason heard apartment doors opening and neighbors calling out to one another, asking if they were okay.

"The vehicle the shooters were in wasn't here when we arrived," Jason said to Lauren as a couple of the officers, guns drawn, started walking toward them, yelling at them to keep their hands up and warning them not to move.

"Agreed," Lauren said. "I would have noticed it. Maybe the bad guys have some kind of surveillance camera set up in the apartment that we didn't notice. Or they could have paid someone to watch the place and give them a heads-up when they saw Matt. Or *thought* they saw Matt."

The officers drew closer. "Just to let you know, I'm carrying a firearm," Lauren said.

"Turn around and put your hands behind your backs," the nearest officer barked at the two of them.

They complied and were handcuffed.

Jason hoped the process of dealing with the police wouldn't take long. Because he needed to find his brother before the bad guys did. Unfortunately, he had no idea where to look for him.

FOUR

Lauren turned the key in the ignition while Jason shut the passenger door and buckled his seat belt. After talking to the police and explaining everything that had happened, they'd been allowed to leave the crime scene at Matt's apartment building. She was still a little shaky from the surge in adrenaline after nearly being killed, but she was steady enough to drive. She just wasn't certain where she wanted to drive to.

She'd been shot at more than once today. Well, technically, Jason was the one who'd been shot at. But she'd been close enough to him to practically feel the ripple in the air as the bullets and shotgun pellets blew by.

Prior to today, she'd only been fired at once before. The fugitives she tracked might hide, lie and get other people to cover for them, but when she finally caught up with them, they typically gave up without trying to kill her.

Today had been a whole new ball game. And now that she finally had a quiet moment, the seesawing emotions of fear and relief were getting to her. Her hands were trembling. And her mouth felt dry. She'd gotten up very early this morning, and now it was well into the evening hours. She was tired.

Not that she would let Jason Cortez know that. Not a

chance. A certain level of bravado was part of the necessary equipment for being a successful bounty hunter. She couldn't appear fainthearted or hesitant and expect to get her job done.

Good thing she had lots of experience making certain she appeared stronger than she felt. And good thing she had experience taking her worry and uncertainty and turning them into prayer.

Thank You, Lord, for Your protection, she prayed silently. *Please help me with this case. And I pray for the safest and most peaceful outcome.*

"Drop me off at a hotel anywhere on your way home," Jason said as she put the SUV in gear and pulled away from the curb.

Lauren chewed her bottom lip for a few seconds, thinking. "I'm not sure I'm going home."

Jason turned toward her. "Does that mean you have an idea of how we can find Matt?"

She shook her head. "It's not that. I'm concerned that it might not be safe for me to go home tonight. The people who are after your brother are still out there. For all we know, they might have had someone watching us the whole time we were at your brother's apartment. They could be following us right now."

Jason turned to look at his side mirror.

"Nobody pulled away from the curb behind us," she said. "I've been watching. But since it's dark, and all I can see are headlights, it's hard to tell if we're being followed. Plus it's possible they could have put a tracker on my car."

Her experience had involved trying to find people. She'd never before been in the position of having someone hunting her while she did her job. Well, the bad guys were actually hunting Jason, because they thought he was

Matt. But the experiences they'd been through today had sort of turned them into a package deal. They needed to stay together until the mission was completed.

"I don't want to risk leading the bad guys to my home," she said. "I don't want to put anybody else in danger."

"Oh," Jason said. "So you have a family? A husband?"

Was it her imagination, or did he sound disappointed?

"My mom and I share a house," she said. "She has rheumatoid arthritis and doesn't get around very easily. Spends a lot of time in a wheelchair." Lauren could hear her own voice turning husky with emotion. The thought of the dangerous, violent thugs intent on murdering Matt Cortez showing up at the house, with her mother there, vulnerable, sometimes barely able to move at all, was too awful to consider. And she would not risk having it happen.

She cleared her throat. "I'm staying in a hotel tonight, too. Someplace downtown with top-notch security and video cameras in the parking garage and common areas. That would probably be the safest option. Tomorrow we'll find your brother and get the case wrapped up."

"Works for me." Jason pulled his phone out of his pocket. "I'll try to call Matt again."

This had to be the fifth time he'd called since they'd hit the apartment and found out his brother wasn't there. The first three times she'd heard him leave a message for Matt to call him back. After that, he didn't bother. But he still kept calling.

It was on the tip of her tongue to tell him to give it up. That his brother was playing him. That the last shred of genuine connection that he believed still existed between the two of them was gone.

But she knew from her own experience that it could take a long time for reality to set in. Accepting the fact that someone you cared about did not care about you came in stages. How long had it taken for Lauren to realize her father didn't really care that much about her and her mom? Her earliest memories were of him being around intermittently. For years she believed his excuses. He always had believable reasons for why he didn't show up for school events or birthday parties or even on Christmas Day.

Then her mom started having health problems. The fever and pain in her joints interfered with her ability to work. And money, which was never abundant, became even scarcer. At that point, she and her mom had *really* needed him. But he didn't step up. Finally, her mom filed for divorce. She asked for child support. The support payments never came, and Lauren's dad disappeared altogether.

Finally, Lauren understood. She'd felt sorrow for her mom, for the sad reality that she'd fallen in love with a charming con man. For herself, she'd mostly felt bitter for wasting love and concern and loyalty on her dad for as long as she had.

Jason took his phone from his ear, hit the disconnect button and slid the phone back into his pocket without saying anything. Obviously his brother hadn't answered the call, and Jason hadn't left a message.

"Do you have a plan for tomorrow?" he asked, his voice sounding flat and grim.

They were in downtown Denver now, near the secure high-rise hotels she was looking for.

"I figure we'll head for the bond office and look through Matt's file. Speak with Al or Barb, whichever of them talked to him and wrote the bond for him. We can work up some ideas based on what they say."

"Isn't all of that information digitized? Can't they send it to you?"

"Facts in a digital file are important. But there's nothing like talking to someone who's actually met the person you're looking for. Sometimes a small detail leads to the capture."

She pulled into the garage attached to a hotel, drove up a couple of levels and parked.

"How'd you become a bounty hunter?" Jason asked.

They exited the SUV cautiously, each of them looking around to see if they'd been followed.

"My mom's friends Barb and Al own the bail bond company I work for most of the time. I do occasional work for other companies, as well. When I graduated from high school, they hired me to help with skip tracing. I'd do some research online, make a few phone calls and track down people who'd skipped out on bills, given fraudulent information when applying for loans, intentionally destroyed rental property before they'd moved out, that kind of thing."

She'd also tracked down her dad, intending to get the child support money he'd never paid. Not for herself, but for her mom. Only that had not led to the moment of triumphant resolution she'd hoped for. He'd passed away three years before she'd found him.

Satisfied that no one had followed them, she walked around her SUV, paying particular attention to the front and rear bumpers.

"Looking for a tracking device?" Jason asked.

"Yes."

Jason dropped down and scooched himself under the car. Lauren squatted beside him and watched as he used the flashlight app on his phone to check the undercarriage. "I don't see anything out of the ordinary under here," he said before climbing back out.

She grabbed a canvas bag from the SUV that she kept packed with a change of clothes and some basic toiletries just in case. Anything could happen when she was chasing a bail jumper, and she liked to be prepared.

They walked through the garage, following the directions to a covered walkway that would eventually lead to the main entrance and the hotel lobby.

"So, the skip tracing led to bounty hunting?" Jason asked as they walked, picking up their earlier conversational thread.

"Yeah. Sometimes the bounty hunters that worked out of the office needed a little extra help. A fresh face to walk into a restaurant and make sure their target was still in there. Someone to knock on the door of a house and pretend to be delivering flowers while getting a quick look inside. That sort of thing. Eventually, I got hooked. It was exciting, it paid well, I was good at it and it felt like meaningful work to me."

"How does your mom feel about you being a bounty hunter?" he asked as they approached the registration desk.

Lauren sighed. She knew her mom worried about her and would be thrilled if she switched to a more mundane career. "She tells me it's my right to live my life as I see fit." Her mom was aware that some of the people Lauren tracked were dangerous and she liked to remind her that it was just a job and that it was not worth dying for, so she shouldn't take any unnecessary risks.

They reached the registration desk and were able to get rooms across from each other on the same floor.

"I don't know about you, but I'm starving," Jason said after they'd gotten their key cards and walked away from the desk. "Do you want to get something to eat in one of the hotel restaurants?"

"I think I'll just relax in my room and order room service," Lauren said. Right now she wanted sleep more than anything.

Jason nodded. "I understand. I'll see you to your room. And then I think I'll get something to eat."

A tired laugh slipped out of her. "I think I can find my room on my own."

"I have no doubt of that," he said, following her into an elevator car. "But I'd like to do it, anyway."

He had nice manners. She liked that in a man. Not that it mattered whether she liked him or not. Because it didn't matter. Not at all.

The elevator stopped at their floor, and he walked with her to her room. She unlocked the door, pushed it open, stepped inside, then turned to him. "We can sleep in. No one's going to be at the bond office tomorrow morning before ten."

"I'll be here at your door at nine thirty."

"Okay. Good night." She shut the door, threw all the latches and then walked over to the bed. She only had enough time to drop her bag and kick off her shoes before falling face-first onto it. The last thought on her mind as she fell asleep was about Jason and his brother. For Jason's sake, she really hoped they'd find Matt before it was too late.

The Gold Standard Bail Bonds office was located in a strip mall along with a barbershop, a thrift store and a coffee shop.

"I've never been in a bail bond office before," Jason said as they got out of Lauren's SUV. He paused and looked around to see if anyone had followed them on the drive from the hotel. It didn't seem likely, but he wasn't taking any chances.

"It's like any other kind of office," Lauren said, also looking around. "It's not a steady parade of creepy thugs coming through the door. Some clients, like your brother, are choosing the life of a career criminal, and to them the whole process is a normal part of doing business. Some clients are decent people who have made a bad choice, and they regret it. Some are actually innocent of the charges against them. People who work in this business aren't judges. We work with the justice system, carrying out decisions that have already been put into place. If an actual judge says somebody has the right to get out of jail if they put up a bond, then they have that right."

Nobody pulled into the parking lot behind them. None of the cars rolling by on the street slowed down so the driver could take a closer look at them. Having a legitimate reason to be paranoid triggered a few of the old feelings Jason had experienced when he first returned home after spending what felt like a lifetime in combat. A little bit of that old edginess was there. And wariness. The compulsion to assess everything ahead of him as a potential trap had kicked in, too. Considering the situation, that might be a good thing.

"I think we're safe," he said.

"I think so, too. Come on inside and meet everybody."

He followed her into the office, noticing the loud beep of a security system as they walked through the door. The people working here might strive not to be judgmental, but they were vigilant. He could appreciate that.

"So, kid, you're getting a little excitement on this Cortez case, huh?" A man who looked about sixty, with the deep tan of an outdoorsman, got up from an office chair and wrapped an arm around Lauren's shoulder, giving her a side hug. "You all right?"

"Yeah, I'm fine. Al, this is the man I told you about

on the phone. Matthew Cortez's identical twin brother, Jason."

Al removed his arm from her shoulder and shook hands with Jason as she completed the introductions. The guy had a pleasant smile on his face, but the expression in his eyes was sharp and assessing. Jason could see Al's gaze linger above his left eye, checking for the scar his brother had, and seeing it wasn't there.

"Al and his wife, Barb, own Gold Standard Bail Bonds," Lauren said.

A blonde woman seated at a desk got up and walked over to them. "Hi, I'm Barb Lathrop," she said. "This is a first for us. Working with identical twins."

Jason didn't know what to say in response to that, so he just smiled and said, "Nice to meet you." He realized identical twins weren't common, but he'd been one his whole life, so sometimes the big reaction got tiresome.

"Come on back and have a seat." Barb gestured toward an area beyond the front desks where a sofa was set up across from a couple of easy chairs. "Let me grab Matthew's file." As she headed toward a desk, she called over her shoulder to Lauren, "Kevin wanted me to tell you he's sorry he can't help you out with this case. His dad is stable, but he's still in the hospital and they're running a few more tests."

The exact nature of the relationship between Lauren and her partner, Kevin, was none of Jason's business. Still, he couldn't help wondering about it. Just how close were they? She'd let him know she wasn't married. She hadn't said anything about a boyfriend.

Barb came back carrying a manila file and handed it to Lauren. Lauren started flipping through it. "Matt Cortez has gotten bonds before, but not through us," Barb said. She pointed to a sheet of paper from a yellow legal pad that was tucked inside the folder. "I jotted down a few notes just in case we needed them later." She glanced at Jason. "After we get somebody out of lockup, we like for them to come by so we can meet them. That's when we take a picture and try to gather a few personal details outside the scope of their formal application in case we need to track them down later. I started doing this job way before everything went digital. Sometimes it's faster and easier for me to handwrite notes."

She turned her attention back to Lauren. "I've got a description of the clothes he was wearing and the vehicle he arrived in. I tried to chat with him a little, get an idea of where he was going after he left here, but Matt didn't say much. Neither did the guy who was with him. The cosigner on his bond."

"Who was the cosigner?" Jason asked. It was likely one of the criminals Matt hung around with. Maybe it was one of the men trying to kill him. It was possible that that was the motivation for bailing Matt out. They'd wanted him set free so they could kill him.

"Tony Santiago," Lauren said. She looked up at Jason. "Does that name ring any bells?"

Jason shook his head. "No." He turned to Barb. "This is the man who put up the cash to keep my brother out of jail?"

"No, not cash. Collateral. A restaurant."

"Santiago's Restaurant and Cantina," Lauren read from the screen of an electronic tablet Al had handed to her.

"Yep," Al said. "I sent you the specifics on this yesterday." He raised an eyebrow. "Maybe you could check your email a little more often."

"You're right. I will," Lauren muttered.

"If Matthew isn't recovered and turned in to the police, we get to take possession of the restaurant and sell it to get our bond money back," Al said to Jason.

"This is clearly the best place to start looking for you brother again." Lauren reached out and rested her hand on Jason's forearm. It was a small gesture, but her touch helped. It grounded him. And reminded him that he was not alone in trying to untangle the dangerous mess his brother had gotten himself into.

He lifted his gaze to look into Lauren's brown eyes. It felt like something passed between them, an understanding. Like this was no longer just a business arrangement for her, which was what it had been after the shooting in the diner parking lot. Maybe she was starting to genuinely care about Matt's welfare and not just about earning her bounty recovery fee.

He broke off his gaze and looked away, not quite certain what the emotion was that he felt. Gratitude, maybe.

"Nobody wants to be forced to give up their business because somebody they vouched for on a bond skipped a court date," Lauren said. "I don't care how close of a friend he is. So we'll head to the restaurant. See if this Tony guy is there, or if somebody can give us his home address. Because I'm certain Tony will want to help us." She smiled at Jason, and his heart did a stupid little flip in his chest. "Let's go," she added.

They headed out to her SUV. Once he was buckled in his seat and Lauren pulled out into traffic, he glanced at the screen of his phone. He'd called his brother again earlier this morning and gotten no answer. And Matt had not called him back.

The deeper he got into the search for his brother, the less any of the information he was gaining made sense. And the more Jason worried that the search might be putting him into even worse danger. Fear for Matt's safety rippled through his gut, and the thought crossed his mind that maybe he didn't really want to help get Matt arrested, after all. Maybe the way to keep his brother alive was to let Matt disappear like he obviously wanted to.

But he knew as soon as the thought crossed his mind that he couldn't do that. Matt had to be brought to justice.

FIVE

Santiago's was a beautiful new two-story building designed to look like the residence on a hacienda with a red tile roof, a painted tile mosaic on the floor in the foyer and heavy, dark wooden tables and chairs in the main dining room.

"Matt told me the money he gave me to invest in the restaurant was earned legally," the majority owner and manager, Tony Santiago, said to Jason. "When he got released from his first stint in lockup, he stayed sober and worked hard for a little over a year. He was living with a roommate, paying modest rent, and he saved up a fair amount of money. He told me he wanted to invest it before he blew it on something stupid."

The thought of his brother getting out of prison and doing well only to fall back into his old ways again made Jason feel sick. And a little bewildered. Why was Matt determined to ruin his life?

Jason had been overseas when Matt's life of crime started. Why hadn't Matt reached out to him if he needed money or some other kind of help? Jason would have come through for him. Did Matt not know that?

He glanced at Lauren. She returned his gaze and raised her eyebrows slightly, as if she were questioning Tony's story. He couldn't blame her. His brother was a known criminal with known criminal associates. They couldn't assume that Tony was telling them the truth.

"Man, you really do look like your brother," Tony said, shaking his head. "It's amazing. He told me he had a twin, but I didn't realize you were identical."

"I don't know how much this building and everything in it is worth, but it's obviously a lot," Jason said. "Why would you put it up as collateral for a bond to get my brother out of jail? Why take that risk?" Matt's legal occupation was long-haul truck driving. Even if he'd saved every penny he earned for a year and a half, he couldn't have invested *that* much money in the restaurant.

Tony crossed his tattooed arms over his chest. He was a few years older than Jason, probably midforties, and the lines on his face and slight bags under his eyes gave him the appearance of a man who'd lived a hard life.

"Santiago's started as a tiny restaurant with twelve tables. I'd wanted to open my own place for a long time, but I didn't have much cash set aside, and my credit history wasn't exactly stellar. If your brother hadn't helped me out back then, at the very beginning, I would not have been able to open for business." He glanced down for a moment, cleared his throat and then looked Jason square in the eye. "I have been blessed. Business has been great. I've obviously been able to upgrade. And here we are.

"Matt told me to keep reinvesting his share of the profits into the business rather than paying him. He never asked for anything. Not until he called me from lockup a couple of weeks ago and told me he'd gotten arrested again. Accessory to murder." Tony sighed deeply and shook his head.

"What did he tell you about the events that led to the accessory-to-murder charges?" Lauren asked.

Jason held his breath, not certain he wanted to hear the answer.

Tony shrugged. "He said his real crime was being stupid. That he didn't know what was going to happen that night. That he was a thief and sometimes a hothead, and he might have been involved in a few things that weren't exactly legal, but he wasn't a murderer."

"That's it?" Lauren asked. "That's all you know?"

"Look, we've known each other for a long time, but in the last few years I've been working a lot of hours at the restaurant, and I'm raising a family. He called and asked me for help. I figured if a judge had set bail for him, then he had the legal right to get out of jail. Innocent until proven guilty, right?"

"And he repaid the favor by jumping bail," Jason said flatly. He was worried about his brother, but he was also angry. Matt was disrupting so many lives, putting people in danger, and apparently he didn't even care. He deserved to be tracked down and locked up. At least until he got his head on straight. "Can you tell us anything that would help us find him?"

"He mentioned he was spending time in Boulder."

"Is he staying there?" Jason asked. "Do you have an address?"

"He just mentioned it in passing. He and I used to go there on weekends before I got married, hoping to meet college girls. He eventually moved there for a while. He said he's been back there recently, catching up with some old friends. I don't have an address for where he could be staying."

"Did he mention any names?" Lauren asked. "Or talk about places he liked to hang out? A favorite bar or restaurant, maybe?"

"No, he didn't."

"Could you give me the names of the places where the two of you liked to spend time back when you used to go to Boulder together? Maybe the names of people you used to hang out with?"

Tony rattled off the names of some bars and restaurants, and Lauren jotted them down. When it came to individuals, he could offer only a few first names.

"Thanks for your time." She handed him a business card. "Please call me if you hear anything from him."

He nodded. "I will."

"And if anybody else comes around asking about him, it would probably be a good idea to call the police," Jason added. "Some of Matt's criminal cronies are looking for him, and they're pretty dangerous."

Jason scanned the restaurant parking lot as he and Lauren stepped outside. Nothing appeared out of the ordinary.

"I suspect that the people who are after your brother are doing the same thing we are," Lauren said, walking beside him. "Checking out all the places where Matt's known to spend time. Assuming Tony was telling us the truth about Matt's connection to Boulder, they'll likely look for him there, as well."

Jason sent up a silent prayer. *Please, Lord, help us find him first.*

"I know this is an old-school technique, but it works," Lauren said to Jason twenty minutes later as they walked into an office services and shipping store a few blocks away from Santiago's.

When she'd first brought up the idea of having flyers printed with Matt's picture on it, Jason had looked at her like she was crazy. "Digital pictures are good, but not always better," she continued. "Sometimes a printed picture, something somebody can tuck into their purse or pin onto a corkboard, is more helpful. If a target sees his picture posted in a store window, that can be motivation for him to turn himself in."

"But won't having his picture posted all over Boulder let the bad guys know that's where we think he is and so they'll focus their attention there, too?"

She nodded. "Unfortunately, yes. But the longer it takes to find him, the better the odds are that the criminals who are tracking him will find him first. There are more of them. They can fan out and cover more ground faster than we can. There's no perfect solution here. All we can do is make the best decisions we can and then act on them."

Bounty hunting was not an exact science. There was a lot of uncertainty. Mistakes were made. Hours were wasted chasing down dead ends. That was the nature of the job.

Lauren got plenty of teasing about what she did for a living. Some of it came in the form of gentle jabs. A lot of it came as harsh criticism. People often asked her why she didn't get a *real* law enforcement job. The truth was she liked tracking down people. And while the idea of becoming a US marshal was appealing, that wasn't a career path she could pursue. Because if she left Denver for training and then traveled all over the country to apprehend fugitives, who would look after her mom? With bounty hunting she could decide how far away she would travel and how long she was willing to be away from home.

She reached the store's service counter. Behind it, a high-speed printer shot sheets of paper into a cardboard box. It took a few seconds for the nearest service clerk to notice her and walk over. A second clerk, farther in the back, was busy packing and taping a row of large boxes.

Lauren quickly sketched out what she wanted on a blank sheet of copy paper, got a destination email address so she could transmit the digital photo of Matt she had on her phone, and then waited for the clerk to make a sample flyer for her to look at.

At a stand-up desk behind the counter, the clerk opened the email with the file image, looked at it, looked at Jason, looked at the image again, and then looked at Lauren with her eyebrows raised and a puzzled expression on her face.

"Matthew is his identical twin brother," Lauren called out over the continuing noise of the printer.

The clerk, who nodded slowly, didn't appear entirely convinced.

"So my brother is basically on a Wanted poster now." Jason sighed heavily and shook his head.

"We'll find him," Lauren said. *Please, Lord, help us find him*, she prayed silently.

"I'm obviously not heading back to Sweetwater today," he said. "I need to make a couple of calls. I want to confirm that my neighbors are still willing to look after my animals. And I need to call my clients who have appointments for me to come out and do welding repairs and reschedule them."

"You can head back to Sweetwater," Lauren said. "You don't have to go with me to Boulder."

"Yes, I do have to go to Boulder," he said firmly. "I need to do whatever I can to help keep my brother alive." He pulled his phone out of his pocket and started tapping the screen.

The clerk walked up with a printout of the flyer with Matt's picture at the top and the pertinent details, along with contact phone numbers, beneath it. Jason glanced at it, shook his head sadly, and then walked away toward the front of the shop as he started talking on his phone.

"That looks fine," Lauren said to the clerk. "I'll take fifty copies. Save the file. I might be back for more."

"Sure." The clerk walked back to her computer.

The high-speed printer finished its run. Now that it wasn't so noisy in the shop, Lauren could hear Jason's voice as he spoke on the phone, although she couldn't understand his specific words.

And then she heard a loud boom followed by another, and then another.

Gunshot blasts! Again!

"Everybody get down!" Lauren yelled as she dropped down behind a self-service copy machine and drew her pistol out of her holster.

Shards from the storefront windows flew across the lobby, the jagged projectiles slicing through the air in a wide arc across the front of the store. The buckshot and debris from the shattered windows caught part of the blinds, ripping them down. Display racks and framed signs and pictures on the wall clattered to the floor.

How had the bad guys found them again?

She heard one of the clerks scream behind the counter. As the scream died down, she heard the frantic, shaky voice of the other clerk obviously talking to a 911 operator, pleading for help.

Jason.

Where was he?

From her vantage point, Lauren couldn't see him. She crawled forward to peek around the corner of the copy machine. She had a better view of the front of the store, and she saw movement, but it wasn't Jason. It was a man striding through the front door wearing a ski mask with a shotgun in his hands. Outside the front door, a large black SUV with a driver behind the wheel idled at the curb.

The shooter stepped over the threshold, ratcheting the shotgun and scanning the store as though he wanted to confirm that he'd killed Jason. Maybe he wanted to finish off everyone else in the shop. Leave no witnesses behind.

Icy fear rolled through Lauren's body, making her hands tremble and finally settling in her stomach. But she forced her feelings aside. Jason didn't have a gun. As far as she knew, no one else in the shop did, either. She couldn't just wait for the cops. Everyone in the store was in immediate danger. She had to do something.

The gunman walked farther into the shop, moving closer to the position where she was crouched down. If she stayed where she was, he'd eventually see her and shoot her. Or he'd step on her and then shoot her. If she tried to move to a different position, he'd hear the broken glass crunching beneath her feet. There was no moving to a more protected position before she engaged him. She had to do it here and now.

Heart thundering in her chest, taking shallow breaths because her lungs were tight with tension, she waited until the gunman turned his face away from her and then she jumped up with her gun pointed at his head. *"Freeze!"*

He swung the shotgun around and pointed it at the center of her chest.

From the shadows beneath the store's shattered front window, Jason sprang at the gunman, launching his full weight onto the man's back and nearly knocking him to the ground.

But the gunman managed to stay on his feet, staggering and shoving the barrel of the shotgun backward, jamming the butt of the firearm into Jason's ribs.

"Drop your weapon!" Lauren yelled. She kept her gun trained on the grappling men, but there was no way she could get a clear shot at the bad guy.

Jason grabbed the barrel of the shotgun with both hands, doggedly hanging on to it as the gunman twisted and turned, cursing as he tried to wrench it out of Jason's hands.

Finally, Jason let go with his right hand so he could throw an uppercut to the gunman's chin. It connected with enough force to stun the guy, and Jason immediately followed up with a second punch to the jaw.

Outside, the driver in the waiting car blared the horn.

Lauren heard multiple sirens in the distance, getting closer.

The gunman cursed, let go of the shotgun and ran out to the waiting SUV, which sped away.

With trembling hands, Lauren holstered her handgun.

Jason walked over to her. He laid the shotgun down on the copy machine next to where she was standing, and then wrapped his arms around her. She felt his lips pressed against the top of her head, his exhaled breath warm and comforting in the midst of all this chaos. "Are you all right?" he asked.

"I'm okay," she answered. "How about you?"

He squeezed her a little tighter. "Never better." Without letting go of her, he yelled back to the shop employees, "Anybody hurt?"

They both answered that they were all right.

Red and blue lights flashed outside. The police had arrived.

"I can't help wondering if Tony had something to do with this," Lauren said. "Maybe he called somebody as soon as we left the restaurant. Described my SUV. Told them we were in the neighborhood."

"It's possible," Jason said. "As soon as we're finished talking to the police, let's go find out."

"We went back to Santiago's and talked to Tony," Jason explained to Al and Barb. "We told him what had happened at the copy shop with the gunman, and he seemed genuinely shaken."

He exchanged glances with Lauren, and his heart warmed in his chest. She was a remarkable woman. Smart. Brave. Resourceful. And despite everything that had happened to them since they'd first laid eyes on each other, she still seemed determined to track down Matt. She was not a quitter. Jason had begun to feel like they really were working together. They weren't just using each other to reach their common goal of finding Matt.

"Tony called his wife while we were still talking to him," Lauren added, directing her comments to Al and Barb. "He told her to take their kids and go to her mom's house. Just to be safe."

The four of them were sitting at the dining table at Al and Barb's house, getting ready to dig in to the Chinese takeout food Al had brought home.

"The police told us that the criminal group Matt is connected to, the people trying to *kill* him now, has informants all over Denver," Lauren continued as she dished some fried rice onto her plate. "It's possible somebody working at Santiago's saw Jason, thought he was Matt and called in the tip."

"After talking to the police, we decided to get the rental car," Jason said, putting a couple of big spoonfuls of kung pao chicken on top of the pile of rice on his plate. Fear and stress after the attack at the copy store might have killed his appetite earlier in the day, but he was hungry now. Life did go on. And apparently Lau-

ren felt the same way, because when dinnertime rolled
around she'd said she was pretty hungry, too.

"The thugs know what Lauren's SUV looks like, and
I'm sure they have the license plate number," Jason continued. "It seemed smarter to leave it in a parking garage
downtown and get something else to drive to Boulder
tomorrow."

"Good plan," Al said.

"You'll both stay here tonight," Barb said. It was less
an invitation and more a command. She turned to Lauren.
"You already told me you were worried about leading the
gunmen to your house and putting your mom in danger.
You can't be one hundred percent certain no one saw you
exchange vehicles, so it would still be smart for you not
to drive to your mom's house."

"I appreciate the offer," Jason said. And he truly was
touched to know that they would be willing to help the
brother of a man who'd skipped out on them after they'd
bonded him out of jail. "But I'm the person drawing gunfire since the bad guys can't seem to figure out I'm not
Matt. I think the safest move for you, and for Lauren,
would be for me to take a cab back to a hotel downtown
and get a room there." He turned to Lauren. "I'll be back
here first thing tomorrow morning."

Lauren shook her head. "No, I think you should stay
here. If you go back downtown, you increase the chances
of somebody dangerous seeing you. It isn't just our safety
that matters. Yours does, too."

Her gaze lingered on him, and his heart beat a little
faster.

"This isn't our first rodeo," Al said. "Remember, we
sell bail bonds. That means when people don't show up
for their court date, we call in bounty hunters like Lauren to find them and haul them to jail. You think Barb

and I don't have a long list of people who want to harm us? Of course we do."

"So we've got good, solid locks on the doors," Barb said. "And an excellent security system. Not to mention vigilant watchdogs who will let us know if anyone tries to break into the house in the middle of the night."

Watchdogs. Jason had to laugh out loud at that. The watchdogs were Daphne and Flower, a couple of chunky and slightly bug-eyed Chihuahuas.

"Don't underestimate them," Al said. "All we need them to do is wake us up if anyone comes around the house in the middle of the night. We can-take care of things from there."

"So you're staying," Lauren said. "Now let's talk about our plan for tomorrow. In his bond application, your brother listed a couple of former employers here in Denver. I think we should talk to them before we go to Boulder."

"Tony seemed like a nice enough guy when he came into the bail bond office," Al said. "But keep in mind the fact that you don't really know him. Boulder might be a solid lead. Or he might be sending you on a wild-goose chase."

"Fair enough," Lauren said. She turned to Jason. "After dinner, let's get started on a list of leads to check out in Boulder. The names of any places or people you could remember your brother mentioning would be helpful."

"I'll do that."

As they continued eating, Barb directed the conversation to lighter topics and mutual friends she and Al shared with Lauren. Jason just listened and soaked up the feeling of family and warmth around the dinner table. It was something unusual for him and something he savored every bit as much as the Chinese food. For a minute or two, he let himself imagine what it might feel like to have his own family around his own dinner table every night.

He glanced at Lauren, and when she looked at him, he quickly glanced away. He turned his attention to the windows instead. He didn't have much cozy family experience, but he did have combat experience. He knew how to stay vigilant. He would stay up late tonight and set his phone alarm to wake him up very early. He would watch and he would listen. He was a magnet for danger right now. Not just for himself, but for anybody who was helping him. Which made it his responsibility to watch out for everybody sitting here at the dining table.

SIX

"I remember your brother working here a couple of years ago. That's all I'm willing to tell you. If you want to see any of his old employee records, you'll have to come back with a warrant. We don't give out information to just anybody. A company can get sued for doing that." The manager of High Mountain Transport crossed his arms over his chest and stared defiantly at Jason.

Jason stared back.

"Could you point us toward somebody else here who worked with him?" Lauren asked hopefully. She could practically feel the frustration radiating off Jason as she stood beside him. She understood that he didn't care if the trucking company got sued for giving out personal information. He just wanted to find his brother. Alive.

But there was a time and place for everything. Sometimes intimidation tactics worked. Sometimes they didn't. Experience told Lauren that the stare down she was witnessing wasn't going to get them anywhere.

"If we could talk to someone who knew him, we wouldn't take much of their time," she added in the most chipper tone she could muster. If they could get the name of a place where Matt liked to hang out after work, or maybe the name of a friend or girlfriend, that might lead to something more.

The assistant manager spared her a glance without turning his face away from Jason. "I don't remember who he hung out with. And it's time for the two of you to go."

"Well, at least we tried," she said to Jason as they walked from the warehouse out into the cold, sunny morning. This was the second of the two former employers listed on Matt's bond application that they'd visited. The guy at the first trucking company had been every bit as closemouthed, too. "And both places let us leave flyers behind. Somebody might call us later."

"I know you're right," Jason said tightly as they got into the rental car. He'd insisted on paying for the rental, even though Lauren told him she could do it and that it would be a business expense for her. It turned out he was determined to be the one who rented the car because he wanted to drive.

Her initial reaction had been to push back on that. She should be the one to drive. She liked to be in control of a situation as much as any bounty hunter. But then she'd thought about the horrible situation he was in. His brother had jumped bail, and people were out to kill Matt. And those killers kept mistaking Jason for his brother and taking shots at him. That was a lot of stress to be managing. So if he wanted to drive, she was okay with that. As long as he didn't think he was taking over anything else.

"Let's head on over to Boulder," she said.

Before they got to the freeway, Lauren spotted one of the big stores that sold everything from groceries to tires. "Let's make a quick stop here," she said, gesturing toward the store. "We need to get you some dark glasses and a hat so you're not such an obvious target while we're walking around in Boulder."

Jason nodded. "Good idea."

They were in and out of the store within a half hour. Along with a baseball cap and wraparound sunglasses for Jason, both of them purchased things they'd need if they were going to be away from home for another few days. Then they got on the highway headed north.

Lauren's phone chimed with a message from Kevin, letting her know his dad was home and doing well and asking if she needed any help.

She glanced over at Jason, who was focused on the highway ahead of them. She didn't know him nearly well enough to know what his normal demeanor was over a long stretch of time, but since they'd met up at the breakfast table in Al and Barb's house this morning, he'd seemed more subdued than usual. Maybe she did need Kevin's help. Maybe it was time for Jason to stand down. It could be that this chase for his brother was too much for him, whether he wanted to admit it or not.

She cleared her throat. "If you've changed your mind and you want to stay back when we get closer to apprehending your brother, I'd understand."

He cut her a quick sideways glance. "Why do you want to get rid of me?"

The bantering tone he usually worked into his conversation was gone. "You all right?" she asked, anticipating that he would tell her to mind her own business. "Because it doesn't seem like you are."

"People are trying to kill me," he said. "That tends to take the sunshine out of my smile."

She exhaled a quiet sigh of relief. *Now* he sounded like himself. Even though she barely knew him, she liked him. Underneath his inclination toward dark humor and his tendency to try to wrestle control of a situation away from her, he seemed to be a kind and compassionate man. She'd seen that in the way he'd looked out for the people at the diner during the gunfight in Sweetwater. In the way he'd interacted with Al and Barb. And in the way he'd treated her and tried to protect her each time they'd been attacked.

So it didn't necessarily mean anything if she wanted to look out for him, too. They were just temporary partners watching each other's backs.

"I won't pretend to understand your relationship with your brother," she said, "but I know you don't want to hurt him. You don't want to have to shoot him."

"I've changed my mind. Right now I *do* want to shoot him."

He shook his head and glanced her direction, a half smile playing across his lips and then quickly vanishing. But even before that, she'd known he was kidding. More dark humor. More trying to find a way to cope with a horrible situation.

"If you don't want to be there when your brother is arrested, you don't have to be," she continued doggedly, because she could tell she'd struck a nerve. She could call Toby and Tim again. They always came through in a pinch.

The ugly truth was that Matt had a significant drug history. He might be strung out when they found him, appearing and behaving in a way that would make him nearly unrecognizable to Jason.

"You don't have to stick with this until the bitter end," she said. "I'll look out for your brother. I'll make sure things are done right."

Jason rubbed his hand over his bristly black hair and then dropped it back down onto the steering wheel. "You sound like you're sure you're going to find him."

"I have to think positive. That's how I get the job done."

"If it's that simple, why haven't the cops already found him?"

"Active, dangerous situations are their priority. It's one of the reasons why bounty hunters exist. We make tracking down a fugitive our priority. Lieutenant Walker at the Denver PD told me when I spoke with him after the shooting yesterday that tracking down the members of your brother's old criminal gang is his main goal.

"Beyond that, the cops have their advantages, and we have ours. They have access to governmental and financial databases. If Matt tries to take a plane, a train or a bus out of town, they'll find him. They can track him if he uses his credit card. They can locate him through his cell phone if he leaves the battery in it. Now that his case has heated up, they'll dedicate more of their technological resources to catching him. We have the advantage that people who won't talk to the cops will talk to us. And if your brother gets word that we're looking for him, he might step forward and give himself up to us. Whereas he might not turn himself in to the police."

"Are you ready if Matt doesn't want to give himself up and he turns violent?" Jason asked grimly.

"If things get bad, I'll call the police, without hesitation. Ideally, I'd like to call for reinforcements before the actual capture. Maybe get Kevin to help. He's good at keeping people calm."

"Doesn't that Kevin guy have some other bounty hunter he can work with?" Jason snapped. The jealous tone to his voice made her heart skip an extra beat.

"The goal is to arrest the fugitive myself rather than have the cops do it," Lauren said, feeling her cheeks warm as she ignored the jab about Kevin. "Because that's how I earn my fugitive recovery fee."

They drove a few more miles in silence. "I keep thinking about what I could have done differently so that Matt wouldn't have turned out the way he has," Jason said.

The raw emotion in his voice told Lauren that this was something that had been eating at him for a while.

"He's a grown man," she said. "And you're his brother, not his dad. You aren't responsible for how he lives his life."

She knew that their father had passed away six years ago. And that he'd never quite been able to pull himself back together emotionally after his wife died when the twins were twelve.

"Of course I'm responsible for Matt. He's my twin brother. I should have done a better job of looking out for him."

Lauren had no idea what to say in response to that. The world sometimes seemed to be divided into two kinds of people. Those who felt a sense of responsibility to others, like Jason did to his brother, like she did to her mom. And those who thought only of themselves, like her dad—and like Matt.

At least Lauren's dad hadn't ever made her the target of vicious gunmen intent on killing her. She supposed she should be grateful for that.

Twenty minutes later they were driving into Boulder.

Conversation between them had trailed off into comfortable silence, and Jason was glad. Because he'd revealed more of himself than he'd intended to when he'd told her he felt responsible for Matt. And that had left him emotionally exposed. A feeling he didn't particularly care for.

He knew that his brother was responsible for his own

decisions. But sometimes logic and reason just didn't seem to matter.

Despite the uncomfortableness of their conversation, he'd found himself wanting to ask Lauren some questions about herself. Not anything deep or profound, just simple stuff. What did she do for fun when she wasn't working? Did she like horses?

Did she have a boyfriend?

He'd started to ask her the first question, and then he'd clamped his mouth shut. Because what was the point? They weren't friends; they weren't going to be friends. The only reason that they were in this car together was because his brother was a wanted criminal and she was a bounty hunter tracking him down. It was her job. That was not a personal relationship.

Today, tomorrow or maybe a few days after that, they'd find Matt. She'd haul him off to jail, and Jason would head back to Sweetwater. He had a neglected ranch that he was trying to build back up. Horses he needed to tend to. And he had his welding business to manage.

Lauren would stay around Denver, moving on to capture the next bail jumper who needed to be tracked down.

There was no possibility of a future between them, and he knew that.

Jason hadn't been in an emotionally close relationship with a woman for a long time. He was out of practice. And he was taking her polite concern a little too seriously.

"I thought of a couple of bars in Boulder where Matt liked to hang out a few years ago," he said as they rolled into town. "After that, we should probably look online to see where the most popular nightspots are and then go there. Matt definitely likes to be where the action is."

"Sounds good," Lauren said. "But before we do that,

check your phone and see if any of his friends have gotten back to you."

Jason parked the car and then checked his phone. Years ago, before he'd gone into the military, Jason had hung out with Matt in Boulder a few times and had met some of his friends. Last night he'd tried to think of the names of some of those people. He'd managed to find three people who he thought might be them and he'd left messages on their social media sites. As of right now, he hadn't heard back from any of them. Maybe he never would.

"Nothing," he said to Lauren, shaking his head.

"Don't worry, we aren't giving up."

Her confidence and optimism were encouraging.

They both got out of the car. He pulled the tags off his newly purchased baseball cap and sunglasses and put them on.

Lauren grabbed some of the flyers with Matt's picture from the box in the back seat.

Jason pulled his phone back out of his pocket, planning to call Matt again and leave another message. If nothing else, maybe irritation from Jason's constant calls would motivate Matt to finally call him back. He hesitated before he tapped Matt's name on the screen. "Should I tell him I'm in Boulder? He might agree to meet with me. But he also might skip town."

"Tell him you're here," she said decisively. "If he is in town and he bolts, there's a decent chance the police will find him. They'll either see his car on the road or track him by credit card activity. On the other hand, if he's in town and decides to meet with you, well, then our problem is solved."

Jason made the call, and of course it went to voice

mail. He left a message asking his brother to meet up with him.

They went to the first bar on Jason's list of places where Matt used to hang out. The bartender they spoke with wouldn't accept the flyer that Lauren tried to hand to him. He barely glanced at the picture of Matt, said they hadn't seen him before and asked them to leave.

"Do you think that guy's refusal to help us is a sign that he's covering for Matt?" Jason asked Lauren when they stepped back outside. He figured she'd had enough experience to know if that was odd behavior.

"Not necessarily. Most people are helpful," she said. "Some just aren't."

They arrived at the second bar on Jason's list. Business was slow. A guy was sweeping the floor, and the bartender was stacking clean glasses on the back bar. She noticed them as they drew closer. When Jason took off his sunglasses, she did a double take. And then stared at him, eyebrows raised, uncertainty written on her face.

"The bartender thinks you look familiar, but she's not sure," Lauren said quietly. "I think it would be best if you talked to her."

Jason drew in a deep breath. Maybe this was his shot, his *only* shot, at finding someone who could connect him with Matt.

"Ease into asking her about your brother," Lauren added. "Keep your tone conversational so she doesn't get defensive. People don't like to answer questions when they feel like they're being grilled."

"Got it."

The bartender placed a couple of cocktail napkins on the bar as they stepped up. "What'll you have?" she asked, her gaze resting on Jason.

"Do I look familiar to you?" he asked. The bartender

had long blond hair and looked like she was in her late twenties.

"As a matter of fact, you do."

"Maybe you know my brother. His name is Matt Cortez."

She smiled broadly. "You sure do look like him."

"We're identical twins."

"Huh. So, what are you drinking?"

"Do you know where my brother is staying these days?" Jason asked. "We're trying to meet up with him, and we can't seem to get connected."

"Sorry, I can't help you. I don't know him that well. I just know him because he's a regular here."

"Has he been in here lately?" Jason asked, cautiously hoping that they finally might be catching up with him.

"He was here two or three nights ago."

Jason exhaled a deep sigh of relief. There was no guarantee that Matt was still in town. But at least there was a chance.

"My name's Jason. And this is Lauren."

"Katie," the bartender said, reaching across the bar and extending her hand first to Jason and then to Lauren. "Nice to meet you."

"Can we leave a flyer with you?" Lauren asked, setting one down on the bar. "It has a couple of contact phone numbers on it. Maybe you could show it to some of the other employees here or to your regular customers. And if anybody knows anything, we'd sure appreciate a call."

"Is Matt in some kind of trouble?" Katie asked, raising an eyebrow.

"We're trying to help him," Lauren said.

As they left the bar a few minutes later, Jason thought about the sad truth that Matt probably didn't have any real friends. Just his criminal cohorts. Or people like Katie, who barely knew him.

Matt needed Jason whether he realized it or not. Unfortunately, by coming to Boulder, Jason may have just pointed a large arrow toward his brother's location. Which meant his search here needed to produce results quickly, before it was too late.

SEVEN

"I think Katie the bartender knows more about your brother's whereabouts than she let on," Lauren said to Jason.

"You might be right."

They were seated in a booth in the small restaurant attached to the hotel in Boulder where they'd be staying for the night. They were eating an early dinner after having each rented a room. It seemed like a good idea to stay in town so that they could respond quickly if anyone called them with information about Matt.

Jason turned his dark eyes toward her. As they'd spent the day walking around Boulder, talking to people and leaving behind flyers, he'd opened up to her a little bit more and asked her some questions. They'd talked about their pasts, about family and about what they hoped to do with their futures.

He was a man of faith. Which, given his behavior and everything he'd said and done since she'd met him, shouldn't have come as a surprise when he'd mentioned it this afternoon. So much for her detective skills. Although, to be fair to herself, she been trying *not* to notice too much about him. She was trying to capture his bail-jumping brother. It wasn't like she'd met him through mutual friends on a ski trip or in a night class or some-thing. This, the time they were spending together, was business.

His identical twin brother was a criminal. Jason could be a criminal, too. Just one that hadn't gotten tangled up with the law yet. Maybe he was a charming con man like her dad. That man knew how to fake emotion he didn't really feel to get what he wanted. Jason could be the same way. How could she tell? She'd only known him three days.

"What makes you think Katie knows something about Matt?" Jason asked.

"The facts of the situation. Katie works in a bar, where people start talking and drinking and often end up saying more than they meant to in public. She sees who comes in, who they arrive with and who they leave with. It could be that I'm wrong, and that she doesn't know any-thing. But I'm more inclined to think she didn't tell us anything more about Matt because she's afraid to speak up. It might be that she wants to talk to Matt before he talks to us. Or she could be holding out until we offer her money."

"If she's got information, I'd be happy to pay her for it."

"Okay." Lauren nodded. "The next time we see her, we'll take that route."

"I've never bribed anybody for information before," Jason said. "How much should I pay her?"

His phone rang before she could answer. He picked it up from the tabletop and looked at the screen. Then glanced at her. "It's somebody who is not on my con-tact list. Maybe it's somebody calling with information on Matt."

He answered the call and after a few seconds said,

"Thanks for calling me, Ray," while looking at Lauren with his eyebrows raised.

Ray Huffman? Lauren silently mouthed the name, and Jason nodded. Ray was one of Matt's friends that Jason had tried to contact through social media.

She listened to Jason's side of the conversation, though it didn't give her much specific information. And then Jason said, "Holly? I don't think I ever met her. Do you have her number?"

Lauren grabbed a pen and a scrap of paper out of her purse and slid them across the table toward him.

"Okay," he said, jotting down a phone number. "Do you know where she lives or works?"

He started scribbling something on the scrap of paper. It didn't look like an address—it was more like directions.

Jason stopped writing. "Have you heard back from him?" he asked into the phone, his facial expression going from hopeful to disappointed over the next few seconds. "I haven't heard anything from him, either. Not since the day before yesterday."

While the phone call continued, Lauren turned the scrap of paper around so she could read it. Then she signaled to their server for the check. When it arrived Jason was just ending his phone call. He handed the server a credit card and held up a hand when Lauren started to protest. "I don't care if it's a business expense for you. I'm paying for dinner."

"Thank you." Lauren gestured toward the scrap of paper. "So, Holly. Is this Matt's girlfriend?"

"Ray isn't sure. Holly and Matt lived together for a short while a few years ago. They split up but still have some common friends. Matt mentioned Holly in passing the last time Ray saw him, maybe a month ago. Ray asked if Holly and Matt were back together, and Matt changed the subject."

"So what's Ray's story? Does he live here in Boulder?"

"No. He lives in Denver. Says he stopped hanging out with Matt a while ago. He told me that all the drugs and the booze and the criminal life had changed Matt so much that Ray barely knew him anymore. But then he ran into Matt about a month ago, and Matt seemed different. More regretful—scared, even. Like something was going wrong. But when Ray asked him about it, he shrugged it off.

"After Ray saw my message to him on Facebook he tried to call Matt a couple of times before he called me, but the calls went straight to voice mail." Jason sighed. "I'm starting to wonder if Matt is even still alive."

"Don't get discouraged," Lauren said as Jason signed the receipt for their dinner and they both slid out of their booth. "We just need to take things one step at a time." She gestured toward the scrap of paper in his hand. "Let's start with paying Holly a visit."

They paused in the hotel lobby, where Jason called Holly's number. He obviously got no answer and left a voice mail message. Then he started walking rapidly toward the exit.

Lauren caught up to him and reached out to tug on his arm. He stopped and turned to her.

"I know how it feels to finally get a good lead after a dry spell," she said. "You want to run wherever that lead takes you. But we need to remember that the people who've tried to kill us three different times are still out there. And now that we've walked through town asking lots of different people questions about your brother, there's no telling what we've stirred up."

"Be careful. Got it," he said, resuming his fast pace.

She stopped him again. And this time he glanced at her with a flash of impatience in his eyes.

"You barely know Ray," she said calmly, looking directly into his eyes. "And you don't know Holly. This could be a setup for an ambush. This could be some of Matt's criminal friends deciding to kidnap you or harm you in an attempt to draw out your brother."

"You're right," Jason said. "Good thing I have experience in approaching a potential ambush. And in dealing with the situation when things blow up in my face."

"That's it, up there on the right," Jason said, relieved to have found this potential connection to his brother. He drew in and exhaled what felt like the first deep breath he'd taken since the night they'd arrived at Matt's apartment building in Denver and he'd mistakenly thought he was about to see his brother. And he'd gotten shot at instead.

The house was white with green trim. It was small and old, with a pitched roof. The thin layer of crusty snow in the front yard looked churned up. Like people had been walking through it or maybe a dog had been playing in it.

"Do you want to try calling Holly again before we head up to the door?" Lauren asked.

"The first thing I want to do is drive around the neighborhood," Jason responded. "I want to see if there's anybody sitting in one of these parked cars on the street watching Holly's house. Or maybe somebody staged at a point a block or two away where they could respond quickly if somebody inside the house told them we were here."

"Good thinking," Lauren said.

Despite the uncertainty of the situation, he felt a grim smile pass over his lips. There was a time when working his way into a potentially hostile situation was something he did all day, nearly every day. When he was in

Afghanistan, he appreciated the skill and the instincts and mind-sets he'd acquired to help him accomplish his missions. When he got home, there were countless, anxiety-riddled days when he'd wished he'd never learned those lessons.

Now, here he was. Trying to find his brother and keep Lauren safe while unknown murderous criminals stalked them. It turned out he really did still need those skills, after all. It was true—sometimes you didn't recognize a blessing until later, when other events or situations fell into place and then you could clearly see it.

He drove up and down streets for several blocks in each direction. Nothing looked out of the ordinary, so he only needed to be concerned about whoever was inside Holly's house. He headed back that way, parking at the curb a couple of doors down so that whoever was in the house wouldn't see them coming.

"Are you ready for this?" he asked Lauren.

"Of course," she said. "But try calling her again first. We aren't the police. She's got no obligation, legal or otherwise, to talk to us. So as someone with some success at bounty hunting under my belt, listen to me when I tell you we want to be very polite. At least to begin with. We don't want to come across as a threat. Not yet. Not unless somebody starts shooting at us again."

"Yes, ma'am." He tapped Holly's name on his phone screen. The call went to voice mail, which was what he'd expected, so he left a message telling her he really wanted to talk to her tonight.

Then they got out of the car and headed up to the front door.

"Don't pound on the door," Lauren said as he raised his fist.

He loosened his grip a little, knocked on the door and

then stepped aside so he wasn't directly in front of the peephole.

The porchlight flicked on, and a voice called out, "Who is it?"

Was that Holly's voice? He couldn't tell. He'd heard her outgoing message a couple of times, but it was very short.

"I'm Jason Cortez. Matt's brother. I just called you."

He heard a couple of locks unlatch. He glanced at Lauren beside him. She wore a pleasant, easy smile on her face. But her right hand hovered near the pistol at her waist.

The door opened, and a woman in jeans and a sweatshirt stood there. Auburn hair spilled around her shoulders, nearly reaching her elbows. Her gaze settled on Jason, and her jaw dropped slightly. "You really do look like your brother."

"Is Matt here?" Lauren asked, keeping a smile on her face, looking like a friendly neighbor who just wanted to drop off a plate of cookies.

The woman shook her head. "I haven't seen him around here in months."

"Holly, I really need to talk to him," Jason said. "I want to help him. There are people who want to kill him. They've taken shots at me because they thought I was him."

He could see the shock on her face.

A child's voice called out from inside the house, "Mom, I want mac and cheese!"

"Be right there," the woman called over her shoulder. Then she turned back to Jason. "I'm not Holly. I'm a single mom, as you can see. I rent a room to Holly because I need the money. Sometimes she stays here, sometimes she doesn't. I don't keep track of her whereabouts. Matt's been here a few times to visit her, but I don't keep track of him, either."

"What's your name?" Lauren asked.

The woman shook her head. "I'm not who you're looking for. And I'm not getting involved in this trouble with Matt Cortez, whatever it is. He chose trouble when he chose to live the way he does." She took a step back. "Leave me alone. If you show up again, I'll call the police." And then she shut the door.

"Do you think that was Holly?" Jason asked as they walked back to the car.

"I don't know. I'm sending the address of this house to Barb and asking her to research the name of the owner. I'll send Holly's phone number, too. See if you can get Holly's last name from Ray."

"All right."

They sat in the car for a few minutes, sending their respective texts. Finally, Jason pulled the car away from the curb and started down the street. He'd only gone a short distance when headlights appeared in his side mirror. He made a few turns, and the headlights seem to follow.

"Are you seeing this?" he asked Lauren.

"Yes. It looks like someone is following us."

He passed through another intersection, and this time the car behind them turned.

"Well, maybe not," Lauren said.

Jason tapped his thumbs impatiently on the steering wheel, feeling disappointed. This whole cat and mouse game was getting tiresome. Maybe they'd managed to stir up enough trouble today to trigger an attack on them. That could mean that they were on the right track. It might be a good idea to stir up a little more trouble before the night was over. And then maybe their search would finally come to an end.

"This is a good idea," Lauren said. "Any time your brother spent down here visiting the bars and clubs was probably at night, when things are hopping. So coming back here at night makes it more likely we'll come across somebody who's seen him."

"I figure it's worth a shot," Jason said.

And at night, with the darkness and shadows, Jason's face was a little harder to see. Which meant they didn't have to worry as much about him being seen and targeted by the thugs who were looking for Matt.

They were back in a stretch of town where there were several bars and restaurants close together. Even out on the sidewalk there were noticeably more people walking around than there'd been earlier in the day.

Jason hadn't said much on the short drive over. Lauren could tell he was disappointed that their meeting with the woman who may or may not have been Holly had not led to any new information about Matt. She'd reminded him that as soon as Ray got back to him with Holly's last name they would be able to find an image of her, and then they'd know if that woman was Holly or not.

Maybe that woman, whoever she was, was too scared to talk to them. Maybe there'd been someone in the house with her other than her child and she was hesitant to talk in front of that person. Maybe some extra motivation in the form of cash would get her to help them out.

They reached the entrance of a bar and grill with a line of motorcycles in front of it and several people dressed in denim and leather hanging around outside. Jason wanted to check it out, because he thought it looked like the kind of place where Matt would feel comfortable.

He pulled the front door open, and the loud thump of classic rock music rumbled out. They worked their way through the bar, talking to patrons and employees, showing them the flyer with Matt's picture. Lauren got the impression that at least a couple of people recognized him, because their gazes lingered on the picture a little too long or they'd exchange glances with a person they were sitting with, but nobody admitted to knowing Matt Cortez.

They left the biker bar and worked their way through several other nightlife hot spots, following the same drill.

Eventually, they found themselves passing by a sandwich shop. They walked in and talked to the guy at the counter. He looked at the flyer, shrugged and said Matt's picture didn't look familiar. They were tired and appreciative of the relative quiet in the shop after hearing so much blaring music in the bars, so they decided to order iced teas and relax for a few minutes. Lauren added a giant chocolate chip cookie to their order for them to share, and they sat at a table.

She broke the cookie in half, took a bite of her share and watched Jason take a sip of tea and look toward the window. They were sitting far from it, at the other end of the shop, but she imagined him holding on to the slim hope that his brother might just happen to walk by.

"Do you have any idea why you and your brother turned out so differently?" She understood it was a very personal question. But at some point today she'd realized that she'd given up any pretense of keeping their relationship on a purely professional level. She cared about Jason. She admired his loyalty and his willingness to take on the responsibility of helping his brother. Even if she couldn't see any possible way of having a future together with him, she still wanted to know him better.

His broad shoulders lifted and fell as he took a deep breath and let it out. Then he looked at her with those dark brown eyes that appeared so world-weary, yet resilient at the same time. She felt a gentle rippling sensation in her chest, like the soft flutter of wings. She couldn't

help it. And she couldn't force away the feelings she had
for him. She felt comfortable with him. Safe. And she
appreciated that he wasn't intimidated by a woman with
her particular type of job skills.

"I've spent countless hours wondering why Matt
turned out the way he did," Jason said. "We were twelve
when my mom died. In my memory, things were fine
with Matt until then." He looked down and blew out a
breath; it sounded almost like a hiss. "But how much can
you trust your memories from when you were a kid?"

"That can be tricky," she said. She'd dealt with that
issue herself when sorting out her feelings about her father.

"Our dad started drinking pretty heavily after Mom
was gone. He came and went. Couldn't keep a steady job.
Sometimes Matty and I were on our own for days at a
time. I did okay in school. I liked to read. Matty didn't
do so well."

Matty. Jason must have slipped into using a childhood
nickname for his brother. It was sweet and so very sad at
the same time, knowing how badly things were turning
out for Matt. A lump formed in Lauren's throat.

"He couldn't go out for after-school sports because
there were grade requirements and he couldn't meet
them. And yet, he was a smart guy and a hard worker.
Now I wonder if he had some kind of undiagnosed learn-
ing disability."

Jason took a sip of his tea. Then he pulled one of the
flyers out of his jacket pocket and gazed at the picture
of his twin brother. "So I was at school most of the time
for one thing or another. After school I don't know what
Matty did. I just know that by the end of high school, he
was already getting into some serious trouble."

Then he looked directly at Lauren, his dark eyes unusually bright, almost shimmery. "I should have looked after my brother," he said, his voice ragged. "But I didn't."

For a few seconds Lauren's breath felt caught in her chest, and she couldn't breathe. Maybe she should not have asked him that question. She certainly had no right to. And yet, maybe this was something he needed to talk about. She already knew he felt responsible for the mess his brother had made of his life.

"You were a kid yourself," she said. "You couldn't have been his parent. Not even if you'd thought of it at the time, not even if you'd wanted to." She reached across the table to place her hand on top of his. He turned his hand over and lightly squeezed her fingers. "You can't change him as an adult, either. He has to want to turn his life around."

"I just hope he doesn't get himself killed," Jason said. And then his phone rang. He pulled it out of his pocket, and Lauren could see the screen. Matt was calling.

Jason answered, quickly telling his brother that he was in danger and asking him where he was.

"You need to back off." The volume was turned up on Jason's phone, and Lauren could hear Matt's voice. "Leave my friends alone," Matt added. "And stop trying to turn everyone in Boulder into a vigilante out to get me. You're making things worse."

"Worse?" Jason said. "People are out to *kill* you. They've taken shots at *me*. What have you done?"

There was a pause before Matt said, "I never meant for that to happen. You need to get out of Colorado for a while."

"I'm not going anywhere," Jason shot back. "You need to go to court. I know you're being charged as an accessory to murder. What did you do?"

"I have a plan," Matt said flatly. "And you're messing it up. Butt out." And then the call ended.

Jason hit disconnect and slid his phone into his pocket. "At least I know he's not dead," he said. Then he looked at Lauren. "What next, bounty hunter?"

"We get back to work tomorrow. We keep up the pressure. Obviously, it's paying off. Matt finally called you back. That's a good sign. Unfortunately, life needs to get worse for him before it gets better. For someone who lives the way your brother does, that's just how things work."

EIGHT

The call Jason had been hoping and praying for came the next night. It was at the close of yet another day spent visiting businesses in town where he and Lauren showed people Matt's picture and asked if they'd seen him. Nobody admitted knowing anything about him.

Ray had not replied to Jason's text asking for Holly's last name, so they weren't able to search for a photo of her. The house they'd gone to so they could speak with Holly turned out to be a rental with the deed held by a corporation. It would take Barb a little more time to track down the name of the tenant.

And they'd dropped by the bar to talk to Katie again, but she wasn't there.

It had been a discouraging day.

They'd switched hotels for their second night in Boulder, because it seemed wiser than staying in the same place two nights in a row. Jason wasn't convinced that they hadn't been followed after they left the house of the woman who might have been Holly. That vehicle could have picked them up again a couple of blocks over from where it had appeared to turn away. At night, in the dark, it would have been difficult to distinguish it from any other car on the road.

This second hotel had a small coffee bar off to the side of the lounge. Their coffees had just been delivered to their table when Jason's phone rang. He pulled it out of his pocket. "It's an unknown number," he said to Lauren as he hit the connect button to take the call.

"Is this Jason Cortez?" a familiar-sounding female voice said. Country music blared in the background.

"Yes, it is. Is this Katie?"

He looked at Lauren, and their gazes connected.

"Matt wants to talk to you here in the bar in exactly thirty minutes."

Exhilaration swooped through his chest at the thought that he would finally see his brother. And then almost immediately it felt like that soaring sensation crashed into the pit of his stomach. Why was Katie talking to him instead of Matt? Something was wrong.

"Let me talk to my brother," he said. And then to Lauren he whispered, "Matt wants to meet up."

"Matt's not here," Katie said. "Not yet."

"Why didn't he call me himself?" Jason asked, suspicion giving an edge to his voice.

"He told me that things were heating up too much, and that he had ditched his phone because he was afraid the cops or somebody else might use it to find him."

"Why didn't he call me on a burner phone?" Jason asked, thinking out loud. So many questions popped into his mind. "How did he communicate with you? And why didn't he say anything about this to me when he and I talked last night?"

"He just came by here, he gave me twenty bucks to call you and give you the message to meet him, and then he left," she said with a huff of impatience.

Jason could hear the sound of people cheering in the bar, and it sounded like the general noise was getting louder. Of course it made sense that things would get rowdier in the bar as the night wore on.

"Your brother said he was going back outside to watch and see if anyone was following him. He probably wants to watch you when you arrive to see if you're trying to trap him or something. All I know is that I called you like he asked me to. Show up or don't. It doesn't matter to me. But you're down to about twenty-five minutes now." After that, she disconnected.

Jason quickly related the half of the conversation Lauren hadn't heard.

"The meeting location is a public place," Lauren said. "That's a good sign. We just need to pay attention when we get there. Be on the lookout for anyone watching us. If this is a trap set up by the thugs who've come after us before, our arrival would be the most logical time for them to take another shot at us."

He called Matt's number. Of course the call went straight to voice mail, and he left a message repeating the details of the meeting. If this was all a lie, if Matt still had his phone, Jason could only hope his brother would care enough to call him and warn him as soon as he listened to the message.

They arrived at the bar without incident and exactly on time. The place was packed, but Katie spotted them and ushered them toward a small table in a corner, where she removed a sign that said Reserved and asked if either of them wanted a drink. Neither of them did.

Jason looked for his brother, but the bar was dark and there were lots of people milling around, so he couldn't see much. The music was loud, making it difficult to have a conversation. But he could see that Lauren was doing her best to scan the crowd, too.

His brother had made a big deal about the precise

timing of the meeting, and yet he was late. Ten minutes passed. Then twenty.

"I'm going to take a walk around the bar and look for him," Jason said to Lauren, having to shout into her ear to be heard. He walked around until he came across Katie. "Have you seen Matt?" he asked.

"A couple of guys just came in asking about him," she said, glancing around nervously. "I don't know if it's just coincidence, or if maybe they saw you come in and thought you were Matt. I told them I didn't know who they were talking about. I don't know if they're still here or not. And I haven't seen Matt, so maybe he saw them and they scared him off."

Jason felt like the floor had dropped out from beneath his feet. He hadn't realized how much he'd gotten his hopes up about seeing his brother until now. The crushing sense of disappointment almost knocked the wind out of him.

And then he thought of the men looking for his brother. They were probably part of the same group that had tried to kill him before without making sure he was the person they thought he was. He already knew those people were reckless. They likely wouldn't think twice about firing inside a crowded bar if they thought they needed to.

"There's an exit into the alley out back," Katie said. "I don't know if going out that way is a good idea or not."

He looked at her and nodded. He needed to take every precaution he could think of to keep innocent bystanders safe. He walked back to the table to collect Lauren and quickly fill her in on what had happened. Then, with Katie leading the way, they headed to the back exit.

Katie opened the back door and stepped outside. Jason and Lauren followed her. The night air felt especially cold after the heat from all of the bodies inside the bar.

It was dark in the alley, with only a little bit of light

spilling over from the bare bulb outside the back exit of the next building over. There were trash cans, wooden pallets and boxes stacked out here. It took a minute for Jason to notice the two men who were pointing guns at him.

It was a setup. He quickly moved to get Lauren behind him. He backed up, thinking they could get back into the bar. He heard Lauren reach for the door handle and try to turn it. "It's locked," she said.

Jason turned to face Katie.

The bartender shrugged. "My help goes to the highest bidder. You should have put money on the table."

Jason felt sick. Of course. This was the kind of *friend* Matt had these days.

"But you know I'm not Matt," he said, confused, and looking to the men lurking in the alley, who still hadn't said a word.

"Yeah, they decided grabbing you might be a good way to get to Matt." Then she glanced at one of the thugs. "Let me get out of here before you do anything." And she disappeared down the dark alley.

Lauren had already drawn her pistol without anybody noticing. And while she very much appreciated Jason protecting her and shielding her with his body, she needed him to step aside so she could fire off a clean shot if she had to.

"We don't need her," one of the gunmen said to Jason, obviously referring to Lauren. "We just want you. Stay calm, don't make a scene and we'll leave her here safe and sound."

They thought she was going to just stand there while they took Jason? No, she was not.

She reached up to tap him on the shoulder and get him to move aside. To her surprise, he lunged at the closest lurker and tried to wrestle the weapon out of the man's hand. The thug managed to squeeze off a shot, and the bullet ricocheted off the side of the building.

Meanwhile Lauren pointed her pistol at the second man, who'd moved into the center of the alley. He fired at her. She felt a stinging sensation in her left arm as she dived down toward the side of the building and tried to wedge herself behind a trash can for protection.

A few feet away, she could hear Jason grappling with the other assailant as they crashed into the pallets and trash cans while they traded punches.

Lauren quickly got back onto her feet, staying low, while trying to find the man who'd shot her. She had to make sure he didn't join his partner and gang up on Jason. She'd taken only a couple of steps when the barrel of a gun was suddenly shoved into the side of her head.

Fear, even deeper and more overwhelming than what she'd already felt, flooded her body.

"Stand up!" the gunman snarled.

Slowly, she straightened her legs. She heard sirens in the distance. Someone must have heard the gunshot and called the cops.

"I don't leave witnesses behind," he added.

He was going to kill her.

She had nothing to lose, so she started to raise her own gun and point it at him. And then Jason appeared behind the attacker, quickly wrapping his arm around the man's neck and knocking the gun out of his hand. The gunman shoved an elbow backward, into Jason's ribs, and managed to break loose of his grip and turn around at the same time. The two men struggled and fell to the ground, fighting.

She heard someone coming up behind her, breathing heavily, and she whirled around, ready to fire her gun.

It was Jason. He must have won his fight with the other thug.

She stared at him as she still could hear the sounds of the two men fighting behind her. And then the reality of the situation finally sank in. It was Matt who had grabbed the gunman and kept her from getting shot. It was Matt who was fighting with that assailant right now.

"Matt is here!" she said.

The sounds of the men fighting stopped. Matt stood up, and Lauren could see that the man he'd been fighting with was lying unmoving on the ground, apparently unconscious.

"Yeah, I'm here," Matt said, in a voice that sounded so much like Jason's. He stepped closer to Lauren and Jason, where there was a little more light. He'd gotten a haircut since that picture was taken at the bail bond office. He was clean-shaven. And he really looked remarkably like Jason.

Lauren could hear the police sirens getting closer as Matt and Jason stood, staring at one another.

"You're late to your own meeting," Jason finally said.

"I called you on my way over here. You didn't answer."

Jason probably hadn't heard his phone ring because it was so loud in the bar.

"And I did warn you to get out of Colorado," Matt added.

This was the point where Lauren would normally get out her cuffs and place her fugitive under arrest. But instead, she watched the two brothers and wished they'd hug or shake hands or something. She already knew that despite everything, Jason still loved his brother. And now, the fact that Matt had showed up to help rescue them proved that he cared, too.

"You were involved in a murder?" Jason asked.

Matt exhaled a hissing breath. "I was there, but I didn't know they were going to kill the guy." He shook his head. "I'm a thief. I'm an alcoholic. I've done a lot of bad things. But I'm not a murderer. The criminals I used to run with thought they could blackmail me into being a hit man for them. But they were wrong."

"I thank God for that," Jason said softly.

"Yeah," Matt said with a slight laugh. And then, more seriously, he added, "Yeah. Thank God." He sighed deeply. "So I'd hit rock bottom with the kind of life I was living. And then I ran into an old girlfriend who'd left me years ago when I wouldn't straighten out my life."

"Holly," Jason said.

"Yeah, Holly. And the daughter I didn't know I had, Chloe."

Lauren thought back to the child at the house. So the woman they'd talked to had been Holly.

"Holly and Chloe came into my life at just the right time. Actually, I wish I hadn't been so stupid and I'd started my life with them sooner." Matt shook his head. "Anyway, when I decided I was done with the criminal activities, my old gang got the idea I was planning to sell them out to the authorities, and they decided they wanted to kill me.

"At the same time, I knew I was going to prison on the accessory-to-murder charges, that I would plead guilty and take any kind of deal that was offered to me. I figured the sooner I started serving my sentence, the sooner I could get out and get back to my family. So, yeah, I skipped my court date. I just wanted a few more days with Holly and Chloe. I never told the people I worked with that I had a twin brother. That's why they thought you were me. At least they did until you got to Boulder and started telling people that you were my brother. And then I had to start keeping an eye on you to see what you were up to."

"Were you following us?" Lauren asked.

"I did after you showed up at Holly's house last night."

He turned his attention back to Jason. "It never crossed my mind that somebody might come after you while trying to kill me. You've got to believe me."

"I do," Jason said.

"And this is your girlfriend?" Matt asked, indicating Lauren.

"I'm a bounty hunter," she said.

Matt stared at her in disbelief and then finally shrugged. "Well, it's time I turned myself in, anyway. I just want to serve my sentence and get back home."

Lauren couldn't bring herself to reach for her handcuffs. Yes, she'd earned the right to arrest Matt Cortez and claim her recovery fee, but she just couldn't do it. Not when she could see the pain written so clearly on Jason's face as he looked at his brother. The police were here. She'd make sure they arrested him. Despite her concern for Jason's feelings, she was not about to let a criminal get away.

The police took statements and collected evidence. Matt and the two bad guys were cuffed and taken away. The crime scene was cleared way too quickly as far as Lauren was concerned, because that meant her time with Jason was over.

Because of the shooting behind the bar, and the fact that their bartender, Katie, was now at the police station being questioned, the bar had been cleared of patrons, and the business side of things was shut down early. The manager had allowed the police, Lauren and Jason to come inside and use the interior of the bar as a staging area so they could get out of the cold while witnesses were being questioned and the crime scene was being processed.

A few of the house lights had been turned on, so the interior was no longer so dark and shadowy. A couple of employees restacked clean glasses on the shelves behind the bar. The manager was in a back office, tallying the night's receipts. Country music still spilled out of the speakers, but not nearly as loudly as before, gentler and more romantic songs playing instead.

The last police officer left, and that was it. The hunt was over.

Lauren found herself looking at Jason. Staring at him, really. Trying to do it without getting caught. Because she wanted to create the strongest possible memory of him. Being the daughter of a man who disappeared with no warning for long stretches of time obviously made an impact on a girl. And the impact remained even when she was a grown woman. You didn't need a degree in psychology to notice that.

Lauren had dated on occasion, but things never went anywhere, because she'd always kept her emotional distance. She didn't want to risk being conned. She didn't trust a man who tried too hard to be charming. That must be how Jason Cortez had slipped under the radar and into her heart. He didn't try to be charming. He didn't even flirt with her. Well, maybe a tiny bit now and then. He had mostly just been himself—a man who cared about his brother even though that brother had disappointed him a hundred times over. A man who didn't vanish when the going got tough.

Did he feel anything for her? Anything real that he might want to pursue?

She didn't know. And she wasn't going to ask. Not when the man had finally caught up with his twin brother only to see that brother hauled away in the back of a squad car. He had enough on his mind. And even though she'd only met him four days ago, she already knew him well enough to know he'd speak up if he had something to say.

As they walked through the bar toward the front door, she cleared her throat and commanded herself to speak in a professional, steady tone. "I'm not sure if the car rental office is open this late. But as soon as we turn in the car, I'll drive you back to Sweetwater."

He reached for her hand. Pulled her to a stop. She turned to him, and he tugged on her hand, pulling her closer, until she was nearly pressed against him. She looked up at those dark brown eyes looking down at her. Her heart beat so hard in her chest that she began to feel light-headed.

"I'm not really in a hurry to go our separate ways," he said, his voice low, the expression in his eyes turning soft. "Are you?"

"No," she answered, as her heart swelled until she was barely able to speak. "I'm not."

A smile slowly formed on his lips. And then he pulled her even closer until she was finally actually pressed up against him. His strong arms wrapped around her waist and he leaned down, brushing his lips over hers, sending her heart soaring as a shiver of delight ran down her spine.

"I don't know how things could possibly work between us," she said uncertainly after the kiss ended and she reluctantly pulled away. "We live in different places. And we lead very different lives."

He offered her a smile that had a little bit of a teasing challenge added to it. "I don't know about you, bounty hunter, but when I see what I want I go after it. A few obstacles in the path won't stop me."

She smiled back at him. "You know what? I'm the same way."

EPILOGUE

Eight months later

Bright autumn sunlight glinted off the gold band on Lauren's ring finger as she packed down the last handful of straw in a flower bed on the Cortez family ranch in Sweetwater. Cold weather was coming. Winter would be rolling in before long, and after that the flower beds would be blanketed with snow. But come next spring, the flowers would be bright and colorful again.

She lifted her left hand and inspected her wedding ring a little more closely. She couldn't help smiling. Her heart felt light and open in her chest. Like a flower in full bloom.

She'd only been wearing the ring for two weeks, so she hadn't grown used to it yet. She still noticed it fairly often. Felt its weight on her finger like a reassuring touch. A warm reminder that Jason Cortez had promised to stay by her side and that he'd meant it.

For several months she and Jason had seen each other as often as they could while he worked here fixing up the ranch and she was in and around Denver chasing down fugitives. At first it had seemed like there was no practical way their lives could ever be joined together.

But they were happiest when they were together. So they followed their hearts. And slowly, things began to change.

Lauren found that she enjoyed spending time at the ranch. Jason built ramps at the ranch house for her mom's wheelchair, and her mom loved visiting here, too.

Jason realized he liked bounty hunting, and he accompanied Lauren on assignments with Kevin and also with Toby and Tim. So in the end, Jason and Lauren balanced their time between Sweetwater and Denver. It didn't take long for both of them to realize that they truly were in love, so why wait any longer?

They got married at the end of August. The service was a small, quiet ceremony at Lauren's home church in Denver. The honeymoon was a week spent in Hawaii.

And now here they were at the ranch in Sweetwater, with family and friends, having a ranch cleanup day and barbecue before settling in Denver for the winter.

Matt was serving his time in prison. He and Holly had managed to get married despite him being locked up. And Holly and their daughter, Chloe, were here today. Jason and Lauren were determined to make them feel part of the family.

Lauren's mom, Anna, was enjoying time chatting with her old friends Al and Barb while they kept an eye on the barbecue grill as it heated up. The three of them were also getting to know the neighbors who helped take care of Jason's animals when he was away from the ranch. Carla, the neighbors' fourteen-year-old daughter, had brought her new puppy, Winslow.

Kevin, Toby, Tim and Jason were just finishing up a

last bit of fence repair near the house. Lauren was finally finished winterizing the flower beds.

"Winslow!" Carla's shout carried across the stretch of lawn to Lauren. "Winslow, come here!"

Lauren turned in time to see some commotion by the tables set up near the barbecue grill. Barb and Al leaped up so quickly their chairs tipped over. Carla took off running around the corner of the ranch house calling for her dog, and she disappeared from view.

"What happened?" Lauren called out, hurrying to the barbecue area. Barb and Al righted their chairs and sat back down, shaking their heads.

Jason and the guys he'd been working with also hurried over to see what was going on. Lauren's eyes locked on Jason. She couldn't seem to get her fill of looking at him. He returned her gaze with a lopsided smile and a warm look in his eyes that made her stomach tingle.

"My daughter's puppy grabbed a package of bratwursts," Carla's mom said. "I'm so sorry."

"Don't worry," Al said, "we've got lots more bratwurst and burgers to grill. Nobody's gonna starve."

But then Carla reappeared around the side of the house, tears rolling down her cheeks. "I can't find Winslow," she wailed. "And I'm afraid he's going to eat the plastic wrap on those bratwurst and get sick. We've got to find him!"

Barb got to her feet and looked around at everyone. "Well, we've got a bunch of professional bounty hunters here. One of them ought to be able to find a little dog."

In an instant the competition was on. The bounty hunters took off running behind the house, shoving each other, each one claiming they'd be the first one to find the dog.

In the midst of the action Jason grabbed Lauren's hand and led her into the stables.

The last she'd seen of the missing pup, he'd been running in the opposite direction. "Do you really think Winslow is in here?" she asked.

"No," Jason said, pulling her closer to him. "I just wanted to do this." He leaned down to brush his lips across hers. Then he leaned in even closer for a kiss that nearly made her bones melt.

After a long, lingering moment, they finally broke apart.

"I found him!" somebody yelled outside, obviously talking about the puppy.

I found him, too, Lauren thought, looking at Jason. And she laughed.

"Why are you laughing?" he asked.

She stood on her tiptoes to give him a quick peck on the cheek. "Because I'm happy."

Sometimes you're looking for something and you end up finding something entirely different. It might be something you didn't even know you were looking for.

Lauren had been looking for Matt, and she'd found Jason. She'd been looking to track down a bail jumper, and she'd found a partner to help her complete her mission. She'd been looking to keep herself and Jason alive while getting the job done, and she'd found love.

There really was no telling what you might find once you started looking.

* * * * *

Dear Reader,

I have always enjoyed a story where the reader is invited along as a hero or heroine pursues something or someone. They can be searching for treasure, looking for a lost city or, as is the case with Lauren and Jason, they can be tracking a fugitive to bring him to justice. Following the hunt is always exciting, because you never know what twists and turns and unexpected adventures lie ahead.

Of course in real life those twists and turns and unexpected adventures can be pretty harrowing. But, as happens with Lauren and Jason, they can teach us a little bit more about ourselves. They can help us to let go of old fears and reach toward new dreams. And they can build up our faith as they remind us that we don't have to go through life completely on our own.

I hope you enjoyed reading *Twin Pursuit*, and I'd like to invite you to visit my website, JennaNight.com, or my Jenna Night Facebook page. You can also follow me on Twitter, @Night_Jenna. My email address is Jenna@jennanight.com. I would be delighted to hear from you.

Jenna

WE HOPE YOU ENJOYED THIS BOOK!

Love Inspired®
SUSPENSE

Uncover the truth in these thrilling
stories of faith in the face of crime
from Love Inspired Suspense.
Discover six new books available
every month, wherever books
are sold!

LoveInspired.com

*On the run from Witness Protection, Iris James can only
depend on herself to stay alive...until a man she thought
was dead shows up to bring her back.*

Read on for a sneak preview of
Runaway Witness *by Maggie K. Black, available in
February 2020 from Love Inspired Suspense.*

Iris James's hands shook as she piled dirty dishes high on
her tray. Something about the bearded man in the corner
booth was unsettlingly familiar. He'd been nursing his
coffee way longer than anyone had any business loitering
around a highway diner in the middle of nowhere. But it
wasn't until she noticed the telltale lump of a gun hidden
underneath his jacket that she realized he might be there
to kill her.

She put the tray of dirty dishes down and slid her hand
deep into the pocket of her waitress's uniform, feeling for
the small handgun tucked behind her order pad.

Iris stepped behind an empty table and watched the
man out of the corner of her eye. He seemed to avert his
gaze when she glanced in his direction.

A shiver ran down her spine. As if sensing her eyes on
him, the bearded man glanced up, and for a fraction of a
second she caught sight of a pair of piercing blue eyes.

Mack?

Mack's body had been found floating in Lake Ontario eight weeks ago with two bullets in his back. This man was at least ten pounds lighter than Mack, with a nose that was much wider and a chin a lot squarer.

She glanced back at the bearded man in the booth.

He was gone.

She pushed through the back door and scanned her surroundings. Not a person in sight.

She ran for the tree line and then through the snow-covered woods until she reached the abandoned gas station where she'd parked her big black truck.

Almost there. All she had to do was make it across the parking lot, get to her camper, leap inside and hit the road.

The bearded man stepped out from behind the gas station.

She stopped short, yanked the small handgun from her pocket and pointed it at him with both hands. "Whoever you are, get down! Now!"

Don't miss
Runaway Witness *by Maggie K. Black,*
available February 2020 wherever
Love Inspired® Suspense books and ebooks are sold.

LoveInspired.com